Joseph Crosby, Isaac Newton Demmon

Catalogue of the Shakespearian Books and Pamphlets

Joseph Crosby, Isaac Newton Demmon

Catalogue of the Shakespearian Books and Pamphlets

ISBN/EAN: 9783741186356

Manufactured in Europe, USA, Canada, Australia, Japa

Cover: Foto ©Andreas Hilbeck / pixelio.de

Manufactured and distributed by brebook publishing software
(www.brebook.com)

Joseph Crosby, Isaac Newton Demmon

Catalogue of the Shakespearian Books and Pamphlets

CATALOGUE

SHAKESPEARIAN

BOOKS AND PAMPHLETS

IN THE

JOSEPH CROSBY LIBRARY,

Zanesville, Ohio, October 10, 1885.

COMPILED BY

ISAAC N. DEMMON, A. M.,

Professor of English and Rhetoric in the University of Michigan.

ANN ARBOR, MICHIGAN.
1885.

NOTE.

—

Having been employed by the present owners of the Crosby Library to make a catalogue of it for buyers, I have had a few copies of the Shakespeare portion struck off separately. There is as yet no published catalogue of the McMillan Shakespeare Library, and I have thought that persons having access thereto might be glad to have this partial catalogue. These titles embrace about half the volumes in the McMillan Collection.

I. N. D.

ANN ARBOR, Nov. 2, 1885.

THE CROSBY LIBRARY.

PART I.   SHAKESPEARE AND SHAKESPEARIANA.

I.   EDITIONS OF WORKS.

1 Mr. William Shakespeares Comedies, Histories, & Tragedies. Published according to the True Originall Copies.
London Printed by Isaac Iaggard, and Ed. Blount.
1623. [Wright's Reprint of the First Folio.] Folio,
full diamond russia, gilt back and edges.
    Fine copy.   London, [1807].

2 Shakespeare As put forth in 1623. A Reprint of Mr.
William Shakespeares Comedies, Histories, & Tragedies. Published according to the True Originall Copies.
London Printed by Isaac Iaggard, and Ed. Blount,
1623; and Re-Printed for Lionel Booth, 307 Regent
Street. 1864. 3 vols. in 1, 4to, half roxburghe, gilt
top, uncut.   London, 1862–4.
    Large Paper Copy, Contains the original "Advertisements" by the
    publisher, and the Collations of each Part. "It is probably the most correct
    reprint ever issued."—*The Cambridge Editors.*

3 *Another copy.* Small 4to, tree calf, gilt edges.
                                                 London, 1862–4.

4 Shakespeare. The First collected Edition of the Dramatic Works of William Shakespeare. A Reproduction in Exact Fac-simile of The Famous First Folio, 1623, by the Newly-discovered Process of Photo-Lithography. Executed, by express permission of Lord Ellesmere and the Trustees of the British Museum, from the matchless Copies in Bridgewater House and in the National Library, at the suggestion, and under the superintendence of H. Staunton. Folio, half russia, gilt top, uncut.

London, 1866.

Almost equal to the original for purposes of study.

5 The First Edition of Shakespeare. The Works of William Shakespeare in Reduced Facsimile from the famous First Folio Edition of 1623. With an Introduction By J. O. Halliwell-Phillips. 8vo, half roxburghe. London, 1876.

"A miracle of cheapness and enterprise."—*The Athenæum.*

6 The Works of Mr. William Shakespear; in Six Volumes. Adorn'd with Cuts. Revis'd and Corrected, with an Account of the Life and Writings of the Author. By N. Rowe, Esq. *Portrait, from the Chandos Picture, in each volume.* 6 vols., 8vo, old paneled calf. Ink-stain on corner of title-page. London, 1709.

"Kindly presented to me by my constant friend, Samuel Timmins, Esq., of Birmingham, England. Oct. 22d, 1879. Joseph Crosby."

This edition was based on the Fourth Folio and contains the seven Doubtful Plays found therein. The pagination of the six volumes is continuous, 1–3324. The full-page copper-plate cuts, one at the beginning of each play, are interesting as showing the stage costumes and appliances of the period.

Nicholes Rowe, himself no mean poet, stands first in that long line of editors who have tried their hand at the text of Shakespeare. His edition will always have a distinct value as an "original source" for the Life of Shakespeare. In "Some Account of the Life, &c., of Mr. William Shakespear" (vol. 1. pp. I.-XL.), he gathered from tradition many details that would otherwise have perished.

VERY SCARCE. Mr. Crosby says, "I was twelve years looking in vain for a set of 'Rowe'."

7 The Works of Mr. William Shakespear. Volume the Seventh. Containing Venus & Adonis, Tarquin and Lucrece And His Miscellany Poems. With Critical Remarks on

his Plays, &c. to which is Prefix'd an Essay on the Art, Rise and Progress of the Stage in Greece, Rome and England [By Charles Gildon]. 8vo, old paneled calf. First fifty pages of text (Venus and Adonis) lacking.

London, 1710.

The arrangement and headings of the poems are from the edition of 1640. Though it was the purpose of the publisher to pass this off as the seventh volume of Rowe's edition, Rowe probably had no hand in it.

8 The Works of Mr. William Shakespear; in Eight Volumes. Adorn'd with Cuts. Revis'd and Corrected, with an Account of the Life and Writings of the Author. By N. Rowe, Esq. 8 vols., 12mo, new sprinkled calf, red edges, neat. London, 1714.

General title-page bound in the fourth volume. Separate title-page to each play, with the cuts reduced and otherwise altered from the edition of 1709. The text differs but slightly from that edition. SCARCE.

9 The Works of William Shakespear. Volume the Ninth. 12mo. Bound uniform with the preceding.

London, 1714.

A reprint of number 7.

10 The Works of Shakespear. In Six Volumes. Collated and Corrected by the former Editions, by Mr. Pope. *Two Portraits.* 6 vols., 4to, old calf. London, 1725.

The title-pages of the separate volumes, including second title to Vol. I., are dated 1723. Pope's edition is chiefly remarkable for its reckless emendations and curtailings of the text.

11 The Works of Shakespear: in Seven Volumes. Collated with the Oldest Copies, and Corrected; With Notes, Explanatory, and Critical; by Mr. Theobald. 7 vols., 8vo, new half morocco, red edges. Portrait by Du-change, but no plates. London, 1733.

"Theobald's Edition of Shakespeare was by far the best that had then appeared, and he proved himself to have had many of, if not all, the qualities of a good editor."—*J. Parker Norris.*

12 The Works of Shakespear. In Six Volumes. Carefully Revised and Corrected by the former Editions, and Adorned with Sculptures designed and executed by the

best hands. 6 vols., 4to, old calf, marbled edges, re-backed. Some plates slightly foxed. Good sound copy.
Oxford, 1743–44.

Though the name of the Editor is not mentioned in the work, he was well known to be Sir Thomas Hanmer, for some time Speaker of the House of Commons. The year after Hanmer's death, Warburton attacked this edition violently. The edition nevertheless became a favorite and was much sought for.

13 The Works of Shakespear in Eight Volumes. The Genuine Text (collated with all the former Editions, and then corrected and emended) is here settled: Being restored from the Blunders of the first Editors, and the Interpolations of the two Last: With A Comment and Notes, Critical and Explanatory. By Mr. Pope and Mr. Warburton. 8 vols., 8vo, new half morocco, red edges, neat. Lacks portrait.   London, 1747.

This edition, like Pope's, is chiefly remarkable for its arbitrary changes in the text. Edwards's "Canons of Criticism" was a rich satire upon it.

14 The Plays of William Shakespeare, in Eight Volumes, with the Corrections and Illustrations of Various Commentators; To which are added Notes by Sam. Johnson. *Portrait by Vertue.* 8 vols., 8vo, old polished calf, gilt backs. Some pages slightly foxed.   London, 1765.

Johnson's Original Edition. Noted for its admirable Preface. Johnson first issued proposals for a new edition of Shakespeare twenty years before. "His preface and notes are distinguished by clearness of thought and diction and by masterly common sense."—*The Cambridge Editors.*

15 The Works of Shakespeare: in Eight Volumes. Collated with the Oldest Copies, and Corrected; With Notes, Explanatory, and Critical: by Mr. Theobald. Printed *verbatim* from the Octavo Edition [1733]. *Portrait by Vander Gucht. Plates by Gravelot.* 8 vols., 12mo, old calf, marbled edges, neat.   London, 1767.

Not a *verbatim* reprint. The Dedication is entirely changed and the Preface is abridged and otherwise altered. "Theobald first pointed out the true road for the illustration of Shakespeare's writings."—*Joseph Crosby.*

16 Mr William Shakespeare his Comedies, Histories, and Tragedies, set out by himself in quarto, or by the Players his Fellows in folio, and now faithfully republish'd

from those Editions in ten Volumes octavo; with an
Introduction: Whereunto will be added, in some other
Volumes, Notes, critical and explanatory, and a Body of
Various Readings entire. [By Edward Capell.] *Medal-
lion Portrait at p. 74 of Vol. I.* 10 vols., crown 8vo, new
half morocco, red edges, good margins. A little foxed.
London, [1767–68].

<small>Capell is *facile princeps* of the old editors. "Theobald, Capell, and Malone,
were the three most industrious, painstaking, collators and editors of the
18th century; and their works, though abused by more showy scholars, bear
the fruits of their patient industry."—*Joseph Crosby.*</small>

17 The Works of Shakespear, from Mr. Pope's Edition. 9
vols., 12mo, new half morocco, sprinkled edges.
Birmingham, 1768.

<small>Beautifully printed and very clean. SCARCE. Known as the "Baskerville
Edition."</small>

18 The Plays of William Shakespeare. In Ten Volumes.
With the Corrections and Illustrations of Various Commentators; To which are added Notes by Samuel Johnson and George Steevens. With an Appendix. *Portrait
by Vertue.* 10 vols., 8vo, old mottled calf, gilt backs,
yellow edges. London, 1773.

<small>Contains the Prefaces of all the previous editors except Hanmer and Ca-
pell. "This edition, in which were united the native powers of Dr. Johnson
with the activity, sagacity, and antiquarian learning of George Steevens,
superseded all previous editions, and became the standard for future editors
and publishers."—*Bohn's Lowndes.*</small>

19 The Plays of William Shakspeare. In Ten volumes. With
the Corrections and Illustrations of Various Commentators; to which are added Notes by Samuel Johnson
and George Steevens. The Second Edition, Revised
and Augmented. *Two portraits.* 10 vols., 8vo.
London, 1778.

Supplement to the Edition of Shakspeare's Plays published in 1778 by Samuel Johnson and George Steevens. In Two Volumes. Containing Additional Observations by several of the former Commetators: to

which are subjoined the Genuine Poems of the same
Author,' and Seven Plays that have been ascribed to
him; With Notes By the Editor [Edmond Malone] and
others. 2 vols., 8vo. London, 1780.

In all 12 vols., 8vo, uniformly bound in old tree calf,
gilt backs. Good sound copy.

20 The Plays of William Shakspeare. In Ten Volumes.
With the Corrections and Illustrations of Various Commentators; to which are added Notes by Samuel Johnson and George Steevens. The Third Edition, revised
and augmented by the Editer [Isaac Reed] of Dodsley's Collection of Old Plays. *Three portraits and fac-
simile.* 10 vols., 8vo, old mottled calf, gilt backs, yellow
edges. Clean sound copy. London, 1785.

21 The Dramatic Works of Shakspeare, in Six Volumes;
with Notes by Joseph Rann, A. M. Vicar of St. Trin-
ity, in Coventry. 6 vols., 8vo, old polished calf, contents lettered. Oxford, 1786–[94].

22 The Dramatic Writings of Will. Shakspere, With the
Notes of all the Various Commentators; Printed Com-
plete from the best Editions of Sam. Johnson and Geo.
Steevens. *Portraits and plates, 96 in all.* 20 vols.,
12mo, full calf, neat, contents lettered.
London, 1786–88.
A sound, clean copy of Bell's Edition, once very popular.

23 The Plays and Poems of William Shakspeare, in Ten Volumes; Collated *verbatim* with the most authentick Copies, and revised: with the Corrections and Illustrations
of Various Commentators; to which are added, an Essay
on the Chronological Order of his Plays; an Essay relative to Shakspeare and Jonson; a Dissertation on the
three Parts of King Henry VI.; an Historical Account
of the English Stage; and Notes; By Edmond Malone.

Portrait and fac-similes. Bound in 11 vols., crown
8vo, old mottled calf. London, 1790.

Malone was an honest, able. and learned editor. The narrow poetical canons of the Eighteenth Century led him into many errors; but his researches
into the literature of the Elizabethan age and the history of the English stage,
have given him a lasting fame.

24 The Plays of William Shakspeare. In Fifteen Volumes.
With the Corrections and Illustrations of Various Com-
mentators. To which are added, Notes by Samuel
Johnson and George Steevens. The Fourth Edition.
Revised and Augmented (with a Glossarial Index) by
the Editor [Isaac Reed] of Dodsley's Collection of Old
Plays. 15 vols., 8vo, old marbled calf, gilt backs, yellow
edges, neat. Slightly foxed in some places.
London, 1793.

Contains the Prefaces and Introductions of all the previous editors.
"This generally called 'Steevens' own edition' is by many considered the
most accurate and desirable of all the editions."—*Lowndes*, 1834.

25 The Works of William Shakespeare. Vol. 7. 8vo, half
morocco. 1795.
An odd volume of the Glasgow reprint of Blair's Edition.

26 The Plays of William Shakspeare, Complete, in Eight
Volumes. *Portrait and 88 full-page copper-plate engravings, brilliant impressions, and generally clean.*
8 vols., 8vo, new half morocco. Ink-stain in vol. 2.
London, Bellamy and Robarts, 1796.

Originally printed in 1791 from Steevens's text. Has Life of Shakespeare,
but no notes. Contains numerous manuscript notes by a former owner.

27 The Plays of William Shakspeare, accurately printed
from the Text of Mr. Steevens's Last Edition, with a
Selection of the most Important Notes. [By J. Nichols.]
8 vols., 12mo, old marbled calf, gilt backs, contents lettered. London, 1797.

This edition was a protest against the "exuberance of comment", so rife
in that day.

28 The Plays of William Shakspeare, accurately printed
from the Text of Mr. Steevens's Last Edition. 9 vols.,

18mo, old mottled calf, yellow edges. Good set, in box.
London, 1798.

Life by Rowe, abridged, and Glossary. Johnson's general estimate of each play is given at the end of each play. There are no other notes.

29 The Plays of William Shakspeare. [Vol. I., containing Rowe's Life, Johnson's Preface, Farmer's Essay, Tempest, Two Gentlemen of Verona.] 12mo, old red morocco.
London, 1800.

Vol. I, of " Harding's Edition." Plates foxed.

30 The Dramatic Works of Shakspeare revised by George Steevens. *Boydell's sumptuous edition, with 100 engravings after Stothard, Smirke, Westall, West, Reynolds, Fuseli, etc.* 9 vols., royal folio, half russia, marbled edges, contents lettered. Some joints cracked. Beautifully printed in bold type, and generally clean; yet a few pages are badly foxed.
London: Printed by Bulmer, 1802.

" One of the best specimens of modern typography." In their "Advertisement", the proprietors say that when the work was first undertaken (1786) the state of printing, in England, " was such, that it was found necessary to establish a printing house on purpose to print the work; a foundery to cast the types; and even a manufactory to make the ink." The enterprise proved the financial ruin of the Boydells.

31 The Plays of William Shakspeare. In Twenty-one Volumes. With the Corrections and Illustrations of Various Commentators. To which are added, Notes, by Samuel Johnson and George Steevens. The Fifth Edition. Revised and augmented by Isaac Reed, with a Glossarial Index. *The Felton Portrait.* 21 vols., 8vo, old marbled calf, gilt backs, sprinkled edges, contents lettered. Some leaves of Vol. I. water-stained.
London, 1803.

Usually known as the FIRST VARIORUM edition. Steevens, working upon the edition of 1793, left this edition in an advanced state of preparation at his death in 1800. Fine tall copy.

32 The Plays of William Shakspeare, Accurately printed from the Text of the corrected Copy left by the late George Steevens, Esq. With a series of Engravings,

from original designs of Henry Fuseli, and a selection of Explanatory and Historical Notes, From the most eminent Commentators; A History of the Stage, a Life of Shakspeare, &c. By Alexander Chalmers. *The Felton Portrait.* 10 vols., royal 8vo, old solid russia, marbled edges, neat, contents lettered. London, 1805.

LARGE AND THICK PAPER COPY. Plates and text clean and spotless throughout. "One of the best reading editions published, and always a great favorite."—*Joseph Crosby.* The small paper copies were in 9 vols.

33 The Plays of William Shakspeare, with Notes of various Commentators. Edited by Manley Wood. *Portrait and 74 Illustrations.* 14 vols., 12mo, old speckled calf, gilt backs, marbled edges. Some leaves and plates foxed. London, 1806.

"An abridged *Variorum.*" Contains Rowe's Life of Shakspeare, Johnson's Preface, and a Glossary. "Mr. Wood is a very careful and trustworthy editor."—*Joseph Crosby.*

34 The Plays of William Shakspeare. From the Corrected Text of Johnson and Steevens. Embellished with Plates [engraved by Heath]. 6 vols., 4to, new half morocco, cloth sides, marbled edges, contents lettered.
London, 1807.

CLEAN, FINE COPY. Printed in large type by Bensley, and adorned with a series of full-page engravings after Stothard, Fuseli, and Hamilton. Known as "Heath's Edition," from the engraver. This is the edition said to have been used by Fanny Kemble in her public readings, "on account of the size and legibility of the type."

35 Thè Plays of Shakspeare. Printed [by Ballantyne, Edinburgh,] from the Text of Samuel Johnson, George Steevens, and Isaac Reed. *The Felton Portrait, and vignettes to each Play.* 12 vols., 8vo, half roan, rubbed.
London, 1807.

The BALLANTYNE EDITION. Without notes. Vol. I. has manuscript index to the 12 vols. "Noted for its accurate and beautiful typography and beautiful vignette illustrations."—*Joseph Crosby.*

36 The Dramatic Works of William Shakspeare: with Explanatory Notes. To which is added, a Copious Index to the Remarkable Passages and Words, by Samuel Ays-

1½

cough. *Portrait.* 2 vols., royal 8vo, original calf, neatly rebacked. London, 1807.

The Index volume is lacking in this copy.

37 The Plays of William Shakspeare, accurately printed from the Text of the Corrected Copy left by the late George Steevens, Esq. With Glossarial Notes and a Sketch of the Life of Shakspeare [by A. Chalmers]. *Frontispiece.* 8 vols., Elzevir 12mo, half roan, red tops, uncut, clean. London, 1811.

38 The Plays of William Shakspeare. In Twenty-one Volumes. With the Corrections and Illustrations of Various Commentators. To which are added, Notes, by Samuel Johnson and George Steevens. Revised and augmented by Isaac Reed, with a Glossarial Index. The Sixth Edition. *The Felton Portrait and Illustrations.* 21 vols., royal 8vo, full russia, gilt sides and backs, full gilt edges, contents lettered. Clean and fresh. Joints of a few vols. neatly mended. London, 1813.

LARGE PAPER. Fine copy of the SECOND VARIORUM. "Vol. 2 has a figure seated, contemplating a Bust of Shakespeare; figure of a man, big, empty, and self-complacent, seems about to 'improve' Shakespeare, whose Bust looks contemptuous and angry."—*Birmingham Memorial Catalogue.* From the "Advertisement" to this edition Vol. I. p. ii, we learn that this "figure seated" is "an engraving of Mr. Flaxman's Monument in Poplar Chapel, to the memory of Mr. Steevens, on which is sculptured his likeness in profile that will be acknowledged a striking resemblance by all who knew him."

"Generally called *Reed's edition,* but Mr. *Wm. Harris,* the respectable and intelligent librarian of the Royal Institution, revised and corrected its sheets, and added some notes."—*John Britton.* Reed died in 1807.

39 The Dramatic Works of William Shakspeare. Whittingham's Edition. *230 Embellishments on wood.* 7 vols., 18mo, full calf, contents lettered. Nice set, in box.

Chiswick: Printed by C. Whittingham, 1818.

Contains Britton's Life of the Poet, a List of detached Essays and Dissertations on the Writings of Shakspeare, and Johnson's Preface.

40 The Plays and Poems of William Shakspeare, with the Corrections and Illustrations of Various Commentators: comprehending a Life of the Poet, and an Enlarged

History of the Stage, by the late Edmond Malone.
With a new Glossarial Index. [By James Boswell.]
Two portraits. 21 vols., 8vo, half calf, UNCUT, contents
·lettered. Frontispiece foxed; library stamp in each
volume.

A fine copy of "The Variorum of 1821." The Editor was the son of Johnson's biographer, and an intimate friend of Malone's. When Malone died in
1812, Boswell became his literary executor and prepared this edition from
materials left by that distinguished scholar. The text is, therefore, much
nearer the text of the First Folio than is that of the Variorums of 1803 and
1813, which was Steevens's.

"The fullest storehouse of English Shakspere-learning of the old school."
—*A. W. Ward.*

"For critical analysis and text-forming purposes the 'Variorum edition of
1821,' in 21 vols., remains unrivalled. It gives a very full history of the
drama and the stage, of actors and plays, of editions and readings, with end-
less notes on difficulties of text, meanings of words, &c., and is therefore
indispensable to critical readers."—*Sam: Timmins, F. S. A.,* 1885.

41 The Dramatic Works of William Shakspeare. With a
Glossary. 12mo, full red morocco, richly gilt, gilt edges.
Somewhat foxed. Chiswick, 1823.

Contains fine impressions of the plates after Thurston's designs. *Whittingham's Diamond Edition.* The play of A Midsummer Night's Dream was at first
omitted, but afterwards inserted, pp. 81-94 appearing in duplicate.

42 *The same.* New half morocco, gilt edges, without plates.
Chiswick, 1823.

43 The Plays of Shakespeare. 9 vols., 32mo, beautifully
bound in full morocco, gilt backs and edges, in box.
London: William Pickering, 1825.
Miniature edition. "The smallest ever printed."

44 The Plays and Poems of William Shakespeare. 11 vols.,
half green morocco, gilt tops, UNCUT. Portrait slightly
foxed; otherwise clean and fresh throughout.
London: William Pickering, 1825.
A fine copy of a very scarce edition. Apparently, LARGE PAPER.

45 The Dramatic Works of William Shakspeare; with Notes,
Critical, Historical, and Explanatory, selected from the
Most Eminent Commentators: to which is prefixed A

Life of the Author, By the Rev. William Harness. *Chandos Portrait.* 8 vols., 8vo, half morocco.

London, 1825.

"Contained a few valuable corrections to the text."—*R. G. White.*

46 The Dramatic Works of Shakespeare. *Portrait (foxed) and vignette.* 12mo, half morocco, full gilt edges, neat.

London. William Pickering. 1826.

SCARCE. Beautifully printed in diamond type. Some copies were issued with plates.

47 *The same.* Half morocco, gilt top, UNCUT. Lacks vignette. London, 1826.

48 The Dramatic Works of William Shakspeare. With Notes, Original and Selected, by Samuel Weller Singer, and a Life of the Poet, by Charles Symmons. *Sixty Engravings on wood, by John Thompson; from Drawings by Stothard, etc.* 10 vols., 12mo, full calf, marbled edges, contents lettered. Upper corner of title-pages stained in erasing library stamp. Chiswick, 1826.

Has the book-plate of C. W. Frederickson. This edition, so long a favorite, is very scarce.

The editor attempted, with wide approval, what Nichols had done in 1797 (See No. 27). "The object then of the present publication is to afford the general reader a correct edition of Shakspeare, accompanied by an abridged commentary, in which all superfluous and refuted explanations and conjectures, and all the controversies and squabbles of contending critics should be omitted."—*Extract from Preface.*

49 The Dramatic Works of William Shakspeare. Printed from the text of the Corrected Copies of Steevens and Malone. With a Life of the Poet, by Charles Symmons. A Glossary: and Sixty Embellishments. Complete in One Volume. 12mo, half morocco, red edges. Slightly foxed. Chiswick: Whittingham, 1830.

Sixty wood-cuts, from Singer's edition. Beautifully printed in diamond type.

50 The Pictorial Edition of the Works of Shakspere. Edited by Charles Knight. *Many hundreds of illustrations by*

Harvey, etc. 8 vols., 8vo, plum colored calf, sprinkled edges. Backs faded, and some leaves slightly foxed.

London, [1838]—1843.

An original copy, with brilliant impressions of the wood-cuts. Comedies, 2 vols.; Histories, 2 vols.; Tragedies and Poems, 2 vols.; Doubtful Plays, History of Opinion, etc., 1 vol.; Biography, 1 vol.

51 *The same.* Imperfect. Contains, Histories, Vol. I.; Tragedies, Vol. I., and two plays (Troilus and Cressida, and Coriolanus) of Vol. II.; Comedies, Vol. I., and one play (All's Well) of Vol. II. Bound from the original parts, in 3 vols., 8vo, half morocco, red tops.

London, [1838, etc.].

52 The Comedies, Histories, Tragedies, and Poems of William Shakspere. Edited by Charles Knight. The Second Edition. *Illustrations.* 12 vols., 8vo, half crushed levant morocco, gilt top, UNCUT, contents lettered. London, 1842—44.

FINE COPY of C. Knight's Library Edition. Said to be even scarcer than the original Pictorial Edition. The type is larger than in Knight's other editions. Has a valuable Preface. "The *ne plus ultra* of all the editions."— *Joseph Crosby*.

53 The Works of Shakspere Revised from the best Authorities: with a Memoir, and Essay on his Genius, by Barry Cornwall [Bryan Waller Proctor]: also, Annotations and Introductory Remarks on the Plays, by many distinguished Writers: Illustrated with Engravings on Wood, from Designs by Kenny Meadows. 3 vols., royal 8vo, half green morocco, gilt edges.

London: Tyas. 1843.

Original edition. Much superior to later impressions.

54 The Works of William Shakespeare. The Text formed from an entirely New Collation of the Old Editions: with the Various Readings, Notes, a Life of the Poet, and a History of the Early English Stage. By J. Payne Collier, Esq., F. S. A. 8 vols., 8vo, half morocco, gilt tops, *uncut.* London, 1843—44.

Notes and Emendations to the Text of Shakespeare's
Plays, from Early Manuscript Corrections in a Copy of
The Folio, 1632, in the Possession of J. Payne Collier,
Esq., F. S. A. Forming a Supplemental Volume to the
Works of Shakespeare by the same Editor. The Sec-
ond Edition, Revised and Enlarged. 8vo, uniform with
the preceding. London, 1853.

In all, 9 vols. FINE COPY.

Contains History of the English Drama and Stage to the Time of Shakespeare (45 pp.) and an elaborate Life of Shakespeare (208 pp.).

55 Shakespeare's Plays: with his Life. Illustrated with
many hundred Wood-cuts, executed by H. W. Hewet,
after Designs by Kenny Meadows, Harvey, and others
Edited by Gulian C. Verplanck, LL. D. With Critical
Introductions, Notes, etc., Original and Selected. 3
vols., imperial 8vo, half crimson morocco, gilt tops,
UNCUT. New York, 1847.

A superb copy, bound from the original parts by Powson & Nicholson,
Philadelphia. VERY SCARCE in this state.

"Exercising a taste naturally fine, and disciplined by studies in a wide
field of letters, he produced an edition of Shakespeare, which, with regard
to text and comments, is, perhaps, preferable to any other which exists.—
R. G. White, 1854.

56 The Dramatic Works of William Shakespeare; Illustrated: Embracing a Life of the Poet, and Notes, Original and Selected. 7 vols., 8vo, half morocco, marbled
edges, contents lettered. Some leaves foxed.

Boston, 1849.

The Poetical Works of William Shakespeare; with Notes
Illustrative and Explanatory; together with a Supplementary Notice to the Roman Plays. 8vo, uniform
with the preceding. Boston, 1851.

In all, 8 vols.

First appeared in 1836. Edited by Dr. O. W. Peabody, of Harvard College.
Based on Singer's edition.

57 The Complete Works of Shakespere, revised from the
Original Editions, With Historical and · Analytical

Introductions to each Play, also Notes Explanatory and Critical, and a Life of the Poet: by J. O. Halliwell, Esq., F. R. S., F. S. A., etc.; and other eminent Commentators. Elegantly and appropriately illustrated by Portraits engraved on steel, from Daguerreotypes of the greatest and most intelligent Actors of the age, taken in the embodiment of the varied and life-like characters of our great National Poet. 3 vols., imperial 8vo, half morocco, gilt, marbled edges.

The Doubtful Plays of Shakspere; being all the Dramas attributed to the Muse of the World's Great Poet; revised from the Original Editions. Accompanied with Historical and Analytical Introductions to each Play, and Notes, Critical and Explanatory: By Henry Tyrrell, Esq. *Illustrations.* Imperial 8vo, uniform with the preceding,

    In all, 4 vols.

          London Printing and Publishing Company, n. d.

Mr. Halliwell edited only a part of the Comedies. Finding that his work was being pirated in England, he withdrew from the enterprise. The work first appeared in 1850-51. Sometimes known as "The Tallis Edition," from the name of the original English publisher.

58 The Complete Works of Shakespeare; revised from the Original Text. With Introductory Remarks and Copious Notes, Critical, General, and Explanatory, By Samuel Phelps, Esq., Embellished with numerous Engravings, designed by T. H. Nicholson. *Chandos Portrait.* 2 vols., royal 8vo, half blue morocco, gilt tops.

          London, [1851–54].

"Although this Work is stated to be edited by Mr. S. Phelps, the actor, yet such is not the case. His name was used, but the work was done by Mr. E. L. Blanchard, the well-known dramatist and author."—*Ms. note by Mr. Crosby.*

59 The Plays of Shakespeare: the Text regulated by the old Copies, and by the Recently Discovered Folio of 1632, containing Early Manuscript Emendations. Edited by J. Payne Collier, Esq., F. S. A. *Droeshout Portrait.*

Royal 8vo, half calf, gilt, yellow edges. Binding slightly marred on one side by a nail. London, 1853.

The "old corrector" emendations exeeed one thousand in number. "This Ishmaelite among the editions."—*Joseph Crosby.*

60 The Complete Works of Shakespeare, from the Original Text: Carefully collated and compared with the Editions of Halliwell, Knight, and Collier: with Historical and Critical Introductions, and Notes to each Play; and a Life of the Great Dramatist, By Charles Knight. Illustrated with new and finely executed steel Engravings, chiefly Portraits in Character of celebrated American Actors, drawn from life, expressly for this edition. *Chandos Portrait.* 3 vols., 4to, full polished calf.

New York: Martin, Johnson, and Company, [1854–56].

"In a letter from R. Grant White to me (Nov. 1869), I learn that this edition was collated by that eminent Shakespearian, though he would not allow his name to appear in the title, or even to be mentioned."—*Joseph Crosby.*

61 The Dramatic Works of William Shakespeare The Text carefully revised with Notes by Samuel Weller Singer F. S. A. The Life of the Poet and Critical Essays on the Plays by William Watkiss Lloyd. *Portrait, from the Stratford Bust.* 10 vols., crown 8vo, half morocco, dark red edges, contents lettered. London, 1856.

Scarce and beautiful edition. Mr. Lloyd's share in the work was confined, for the most part, to the Biographical Sketch and the able Critical Essays appended to the several plays.

62 The Works of William Shakespeare. The Text revised by the Rev. Alexander Dyce. *Portrait, from the Monument at Stratford.* 6 vols., 8vo, new half morocco, marbled edges, contents lettered. London, 1857.

Fine copy of Dyce's First Edition. In type and paper this edition is superior to subsequent editions by the same editor. The text is also more conservative.

63 Shakespeare's Comedies, Histories, Tragedies, and Poems. Edited by J. Payne Collier, Esq., F. S. A. The Second

Edition. *Droeshout Portrait.* 6 vols., 8vo, half morocco, gilt top, *uncut*, contents lettered.

London, 1858.

Contains the History of the Stage and Life of Shakespeare revised from the first Edition (See No. 54); also a new Preface (34 pp.), Index to the Life (12 pp.), etc. "No faithful scholar of Shakespeare can omit studying Collier." —*Joseph Crosby.*

64 The Plays of Shakespeare. Edited by Howard Staunton. The Illustrations by John Gilbert. Engraved by the Brothers Dalziel. *Portrait, from the Stratford Bust.* 3 vols., royal 8vo, half morocco, full gilt edges.

London, 1858–60.

Original edition, with brilliant impressions of the numerous wood-cuts. Though entitled "The Plays," the Poems are found at the end of Vol. III. "This edition is extensively and deservedly admired by all, scholar, critic, and general reader."—*Joseph Crosby.*

Inserted in Vol. I. is an eight-page autograph letter from the editor to Mr. Crosby, touching the so-called "Library Edition" of the work, and other matters.

65 The Works of William Shakespeare The Plays edited from the Folio of MDCXXIII, with Various Readings from all the Editions and all the Commentators, Notes, Introductory Remarks, a Historical Sketch of the Text, an Account of the Rise and Progress of the English Drama, a Memoir of the Poet, and an Essay upon his Genius By Richard Grant White. *The Felton Portrait and facsimiles.* 12 vols., crown 8vo. Solidly bound in half green morocco, marbled edges. London, 1859–65.

This copy contains, throughout, numerous textual notes in pencil by Mr. Crosby.

66 Chambers's Household Edition of the Dramatic Works of William Shakespeare. Edited by R. Carruthers and W. Chambers. Illustrated by Keeley Halswelle. *Portrait.* 10 vols., crown 8vo, half levant morocco, gilt tops, *uncut.* London and Edinburgh, 1861–63.

An elegant set. A Family Edition. "Objectionable words and phrases are omitted, and occasionally a word is substituted—marked by inverted commas—where the sense or harmony of the passage would be rendered defective by the elision."—*Extract from the Preface.*

2

67 The Works of Shakespeare: the Text carefully restored according to the First Editions: with Introductions, Notes original and selected, and a Life of the Poet; by the Rev. H. N. Hudson, A. M. *Chandos Portrait.* 11 vols., crown 8vo, half yellow calf, marbled edges, contents lettered. Boston, 1863–64.

First published 1851-56. Based on Singer's celebrated Chiswick edition, 1826. The notes by the American editor are signed " H."

68 The Works of William Shakespeare edited [Vol. I.] by William George Clark and John Glover, [other vols.] by William George Clark and William Aldis Wright. 9 vols., 8vo, half morocco, gilt tops, *uncut*, contents lettered. Cambridge and London, 1863–66.

The noted "Cambridge Shakespeare," now SCARCE. Indispensable to the critical student of Shakespeare's text. Pencil notes in margins by Mr. Crosby.

"The appearance, in 1863, of the so-called Cambridge Edition created an era in Shakespearian literature, and put all students of Shakespeare's text in debt to the learned and laborious Editors."—*Horace Howard Furness.*

69 The Reference Shakspere: A Memorial Edition of Shakspere's Plays, containing Eleven Thousand Six Hundred References. Compiled by John B. Marsh, Manchester. *Jansen Portrait.* Royal 8vo, half morocco, gilt edges. London, 1864.

On the plan of the Reference Bible, the ₁object being " to make Shakspere self-interpretative."

70 The Works of William Shakespeare Edited, with a Scrupulous Revision of the Text, by Charles and Mary Cowden Clarke. *Droeshout Portrait.* 4 vols., 8vo, tree calf gilt, marbled edges, contents lettered.

London, 1864.

An elegant set. Contains a full Glossary, " with references of Act and Scene to each passage," but no notes.

71 The Complete Works of Shakespeare: including the Whole of the Plays and Poems. With a Memoir and Essay on his Genius, by Barry Cornwall. Illustrated with Steel Engravings. Thick volume, pp. 955, half green morocco, gilt back and edges.

London and New York, [1864].

Known as the "Commemoration Edition." " A most creditable as well as pretty edition."—*Joseph Crosby.*

72 The Works of William Shakespeare. The Text Revised
by the Rev. Alexander Dyce. Second Edition. *Two
portraits, (Stratford Bust and Droeshout)*. 8 vols.,
8vo, half morocco, gilt tops, *uncut*, contents lettered.
London, 1864–67.

Some pencil notes in the margins by Mr. Crosby. "The present work is so
far from being a reprint of the edition which appeared in 1857, that it exhibits
a text altered and amended from beginning to end........I would fain hope that,
in ceasing to be a timid editor, I have not become a rash one."—*Author's
Preface.*

The Ninth Volume is composed entirely of a Glossary of 514 pages, containing uncommon words, obscure passages, proverbial expressions, cant phrases,
etc., etc.

73 Cassell's Illustrated Shakespeare. The Plays of Shakespeare. Edited and Annotated by Charles and Mary
Cowden Clarke. Illustrated by H. C. Selous. 3 vols.,
4to, half turkey morocco, gilt tops, *uncut*.
London, [1865–69].

FINE COPY. On a different plan from the earlier editions by the same
editors. This edition is skilfully expurgated and fully annotated for "younger
and more unaccustomed students of Shakespeare."

Inserted in Vol. I. is an original sonnet by Mary Cowden Clarke, entitled
"Sick-bed Reflection," in the hand-writing of her husband.

74 The Globe Edition. The Works of William Shakespeare
edited by William George Clark and William Aldis
Wright. Crown 8vo, full morocco, red edges.
Boston (Cambridge), 1866.

First appeared in 1865. From the excellence of the text and the fact of the
lines' being numbered, it is the edition generally cited by recent editors.

75 The Plays of William Shakespeare. Carefully edited by
Thomas Keightley. *Marshall Portrait*. 6 vols., post
8vo, half russia, gilt tops, contents lettered.
Boston (London), 1866.

76 Dicks' Complete Edition of Shakspere's Works. With
Thirty-seven Illustrations, and a Memoir. Crown 8vo,
new half morocco, sprinkled edges. London, [1866?].
Published at one shilling in paper covers, and widely sold.

77 The Handy-Volume Shakspeare. 13 vols., 16mo, half
morocco, gilt, contents lettered. London, 1866–67.
Short preface signed "Q. D." No notes.

78 The Stratford Shakspere. Edited by Charles Knight.
  Portrait. 6 vols., crown 8vo, half morocco, gilt tops,
  uncut. London, 1867.
  First appeared in this form in 1854-56. Designed as "The People's Shakspere." Contains Life of Shakspere and Notice of Editions, and brief notes
  at end of each play.

79 Blackfriar's Edition. The Works of William Shakspere.
  Edited by Charles Knight. Crown 8vo, half green
  morocco, marbled edges. London, 1867.
  Text the same as in Knight's Revised "Pictorial Shakspere."

80 "Chandos Classics." The Works of William Shakspeare.
  Life, Glossary, &c. Reprinted from the Original Edition, and Compared with all recent Commentators.
  16mo, half blue morocco, marbled edges.
  London, 1868.

81 The Dramatic Works of William Shakespeare with Copi-
  ous Glossarial Notes and Biographical Notice. By
  Robert Inglis. Four Engravings on Steel. Small 8vo,
  full red morocco, gilt edges.
  Edinburgh and London, [1871].
  Slightly expurgated for family use.

82 The Dramatic Works of William Shakspeare, from the
  Text of Johnson, Stevens, and Reed, with Glossarial
  Notes, Life, &c. A New Edition, by William Hazlitt,
  Esq. 4 vols.

  The Supplementary Works of William Shakspeare, comprising his Poems and Doubtful Plays; with Glossarial
  and other Notes. A New Edition, by William Hazlitt,
  Esq. 1 vol. In all, 5 vols., small 8vo, half leatherette,
  gilt tops, uncut, new, contents lettered.
  London, [1871].
  The first edition appeared in 1851, and the New Edition the next year.

83 The Complete Works of William Shakespeare, with a
  Life of the Poet; Glossarial and other Notes, etc., etc.,
  from the Works of Collier, Knight, Dyce, Douce, Hal-

liwell, Hunter, Richardson, Verplanck, and Hudson.
Edited by George Long Duyckinck. Royal 8vo, full
morocco, gilt edges. Philadelphia, 1872.

84 The Globe Edition. The Works of William Shakespeare
edited by William George Clark and William Aldis
Wright. Crown 8vo, new half calf, gilt, marbled edges.
London, 1873.

The same as No. 74, except date.

85 The Dramatic Works of William Shakespeare. With
Biographical Introduction, by Henry Glassford Bell.
Portrait, from Stratford Bust. 6 vols., small 8vo, red
cloth. London and Glasgow, 1875.

86 The Works of William Shakespeare. The Text carefully
revised by the Rev. Alexander Dyce. Third Edition.
Droeshout Portrait. 9 vols., 8vo, half turkey morocco,
gilt tops, uncut, contents lettered. London, 1875–76.

FINE COPY. Edited by John Forster from material committed to him by
Mr. Dyce shortly before his death. The changes from the Second Edition are
chiefly in the first four volumes. Dyce's text is in very high esteem.

87 The Works of Shakspere Imperial Edition Edited by
Charles Knight With Illustrations on Steel. *Chandos
Portrait.* 2 vols., folio, half levant morocco, full gilt
edges.
London and New York: Virtue & Co., [1875–77].

A reprint of Knight's Second Pictorial Edition, without the wood-cuts, but
containing 50 full-page steel engravings after Cope, Maclise, Mulready, Leslie,
Boughton, and others. Presented to Mr. Crosby by the publishers. A fine
copy.

88 The Leopold Shakspere. The Poet's Works, in Chronological Order, from the Text of Professor Delius. With
" The Two Noble Kinsmen" and " Edward III.," and
an Introduction by F. J. Furnivall. Illustrated. *Portrait.* Small 4to, half dark turkey morocco, red edges.
London, Paris, and New York, [1877].

Dedicated to Prince Leopold. youngest son of Queen Victoria, and named
from him. Furnivall's Introduction of 120 pages (not printed separately) is
highly valued.

80. The Works of William Shakespeare. From the Text of
Clark and Wright. With a Copious Glossary. To which
is added an Index to familiar Passages, and an Index to
the Characters in each Play. American Edition. *Chandos Portrait.* 8vo, cloth, gilt edges.

New York: Crowell, [1878].

Presented to Mr. Crosby by the publisher. A verbatim reprint of the Globe
Edition (See No. 74).

90 *The same.* On smaller paper. 12mo, cloth, gilt edges.

91 The Plays and Poems of William Shakespeare, with the
Purest Text and the Briefest Notes. Edited by J.
Payne Collier. 8 vols., small 4to, half morocco, leather-
ette sides, red tops, UNCUT, contents lettered.

London: Privately Printed for the Subscribers. 1878.

Each play is paged separately. " King Edward the Tnird" is inserted in its
place, and with it is bound (Vol. III.) a pamphlet of sixteen pages by the
author, entitled, "King Edward the Third, a Historical Play by William
Shakespeare" in which he contends for Shakespeare's authorship of the play.
(Dated " Maidenhead, March 14th, 1884.") This pamphlet contains the inscription, "To Joseph Crosby Esqr from J. Payne Collier 8 May 1876". "Pericles,"
" The Two Noble Kinsmen," ." A Yorkshire Tragedy" and " Mucedorus," are
also included. It was not the original purpose of the author to include the
Poems, but in deference to the wishes of his subscribers he added them in
the eighth volume.

EXTREMELY SCARCE. Only fifty-eight sets were issued. The first proposals were for fifty subscribers; but the expense of printing exceeding the
estimate, eight additional subscribers were taken by the editor in order "to
recoup himself."

"As to the text, I have been guided, and indeed governed, by a close examination of, I may say, every authentic impression that has been issued from the
year 1590 to the present day........I began my own researches much before I was
nineteen, and I have continued them industriously until now, when, in my
90th year, I can safely assert that there is no play, and no passage in a play, by
Shakespeare, regarding which I have not read, and carefully weighed, every
argument that has been advanced.......If, therefore, in any case a decision of
mine may seem erroneous, I have arrived at it after long study and delibera-
tion, and with a sincere desire not to cavil, but to be right."—*Extract from
Preface.*

92 The "Arundel Poets." The Complete Works of William
Shakespeare. Arranged in their Chronological Order.
Edited by W. G. Clark and W. Aldis Wright. With an
Introduction to each play, adapted from the Shakes-

pearean Primer of Professor Dowden. Illustrated by
John Gilbert, R. A. *Droeshout Portrait.* Thick crown
8vo, cloth, gilt edges. New York, [1879].
A reproduction of the Globe Edition (No. 74) in larger type.

93 The Howard Shakspeare. Shakspeare's Dramatic Works.
With Explanatory Notes, parallel Passages, historical
and critical Illustrations, a copious Glossary, biographi-
cal Sketch, and Indexes, By W. H. Davenport Adams.
With 370 Illustrations by the late Frank Howard.
Thick crown 8vo, cloth, gilt back and edges.
London, 1879.

94 Shakespeare's Complete Works. Fine Avon Edition.
Portrait. 2 vols. in 1, royal 8vo, half turkey morocco,
gilt edges. Philadelphia, 1880.
Title from back. This is probably the best American Edition of Shakespeare in one volume.

95 The Complete Works of William Shakespeare. With a
Life of the Poet, explanatory Foot-notes, critical Notes,
and a Glossarial Index. ˙ Harvard Edition. By the Rev.
Henry N. Hudson, LL. D. *The Felton Portrait.* 20
vols., 12mo, full morocco, red tops, contents lettered.
Interleaved. Boston, 1881.
"To Mr. Joseph ¡Crosby, in heart-felt acknowledgment of his learned and
judicious help towards making the *Harvard Shakespeare* what it is: from his
obliged and grateful friend, Henry N. Hudson. Cambridge, April 10, 1882."
Contains manuscript notes by Mr. Crosby.

96 Shakspere's Works. 5 vols., post 8vo, white parchment,
gilt tops, uncut. London, 1882.
Vols. I. to V. of the beautifully printed Parchment Library edition. The
text is Delius's.

97 Mr. William Shakespeare's Comedies Histories Tragedies
and Poems The Text newly edited with Glossarial
Historical and Explanatory Notes by Richard Grant
White. *Portrait, from the Stratford Bust.* 3 vols.,
crown 8vo, cloth, gilt tops, uncut. Boston, 1883.
The Riverside Shakespeare, designed for general readers,

II. SELECTIONS, SEPARATE PLAYS, AND POEMS.

98 Twenty of the Plays of Shakespeare, Being the whole
Number printed in Quarto During his Life-time, or
before the Restoration, Collated where there were different Copies, and Publish'd from the Originals, by George
Steevens, Esq. 4 vols., 8vo, old calf, gilt backs. Clean
copy.   London, 1766.
"Most accurately did he execute this laborious duty."—*Charles Knight.*

99 Henry V., 1608; Titus Andronicus, 1611. Two plays from
the preceding, bound separately, in half morocco, neat.
2 vols., [London, 1766].
" Mr. Joseph Crosby Esqr from his sincere friend and well-wisher W. Leighton Jr. April 23, 1881."

100 The First Edition of the Tragedy of Hamlet, by Will-
iam Shakespeare. London. Printed for N. L. (Nicho-
las Ling) and John Trundell 1603. Reprinted at the ·
Shakespeare Press, by William Nicol, for Payne and
Foss, Pall Mall. 1825. 8vo, half morocco, gilt top.
"To Joseph Crosby Esqr from his sincere friend and well-wisher W.
Leighton Jr. April 23, 1881."

101 Hamlet By William Shake-speare, 1603; Hamlet By
William Shakespeare, 1604: Being exact Reprints of
the First and Second Editions of Shakespeare's great
Drama, from the very rare Originals in the possession
of his Grace the Duke of Devonshire; with the two
texts printed on opposite pages, and so arranged that
the parallel passages face each other. And a Biographical Preface by Samuel Timmins. 8vo, half
morocco, gilt top, uncut.   London, 1860.

102 Much adoe about Nothing. As it hath been sundrie
times publikely acted by the right honourable, the

Lord Chamberlaine his servants. Written by William Shakespeare. London, 1600. 8vo, half morocco, uncut.

Staunton's Photo-lithographic Facsimile, London, 1804.

103 Shakespeare's Sonnets, and a Lover's Complaint. Reprinted in the Orthography, and Punctuation of the original edition of 1609. 8vo, cloth, uncut.

London, 1870.

104 Shakspere Quarto Facsimiles, executed under the superintendence of F. J. Furnivall, Esq., Founder and Director of the New Shakspere Society, by Mr. W. Griggs. Nos. 1 to 10, as follows: Hamlet, 1603; Hamlet, 1604; Mid. Night's Dream, 1600 (Fisher); Mid. Night's Dream, 1600 (Roberts); Loves Labors Lost, 1598; Merchant of Venice, 1600 (Roberts); Merry Wives, 1602; Henry IV., Part I., 1598; Henry IV., Part II., 1600; The Passionate Pilgrim, 1599. 4to, half morocco. London, [1879–83].

The importance of the Quartos in determining the text of Shakespeare can hardly be overestimated. The originals of the above, if they could be obtained at all, would cost many hundreds of dollars.

105 *A duplicate copy of No. 10.* The Passionate Pilgrim, 1599. 4to, half morocco. London, [1883].

106 King Lear. A Tragedy. By William Shakespeare. Collated with the Old and Modern Editions. 8vo.

London, 1770.

Othello, the Moor of Venice. A Tragedy. By William Shakespeare. Collated with the Old and Modern Editions. 8vo. London, 1773.

The two newly bound in one volume, half morocco, red edges.

Charles Jennens, the editor of these plays, proposed to edit the whole of Shakespeare's dramatic works on this scale; but he published only five plays. The other three were Hamlet, Macbeth, and Julius Caesar.

107 *Odd Volume of Plays.* Bell's Acting Edition. 12mo, new half morocco.

Contains: Coriolanus, 1773; Dryden's All for Love, 1782; Otway's The Orphan, 1780.

108 Macbeth: A Tragedy. Written by William Shakspeare. With Notes and Emendations, by Harry Rowe, Trumpet-Major to the High Sheriffs of Yorkshire; and Master of a Puppet-Show. The Second Edition. 8vo, half red morocco. York, 1799.

SCARCE. The real editor was one Alexander Hunter, M. D. " Not choosing to acknowledge it publicly, he gave it to Harry Rowe to publish it for his own emolument." Fee " Notes and Queries," May 2ʰ, 1867; and Furness's Variorum Macbeth, pp, ix, x. A comic portrait of Rowe, "Manager Commenced Author," forms a frontispiece to the volume.

109 The Plays of William Shakspeare. *Thirteen parts*: Hamlet, Merchant, Macbeth, Othello, Romeo and Juliet, Much Ado, As You Like It, Winters Tale, Merry Wives, Twelfth Night, Midsummer-Night's Dream, 1 Henry IV.; 2 Henry IV. 13 vols., 8vo, old half calf, uncut. [London, 1803–5.]

Separate parts of WALLIS and SCHOLEY'S Edition.

110 Hamlet, and As You Like It. A Specimen of a New Edition of Shakespeare. By Thomas Caldecott, Esq. 8vo, full leather, red edges. London, 1820.

Adheres closely to the First Folio. This "Specimen" appeared again with some changes in 1832; but the editor did not carry his project farther.

111 *Odd volume of Plays.* Cumberland's Acting Edition. 12mo, half morocco. London, [about 1828].

The Plays are: 2 Gentlemen, T. N., All's Well, Winter's Tale, and Meas. for Meas. (Dolby's British Theatre).

112 Hamlet, and As You Like It. A Specimen of an Edition of Shakespeare. By Thomas Caldecott, Esq. 8vo. half morocco, gilt, *uncut*. London, 1832.

FINE COPY. See note to No. 110. The work was privately printed. in an edition of 250 copies, and was never offered for sale.

113 A Supplement to the Plays of William Shakspeare: Comprising the Seven Dramas, which have been ascribed to his Pen, but which are not included with his writings in modern Editions. Edited with Notes, and an Introduction to each Play, by William Gilmore Simms, Esq. The First American Edition. 8vo, original red cloth, gilt. New York, 1848.

A second volume of " imputed plays " was projected by the publishers, but was never issued.

114 Shakespeare Restored. Macbeth. [Edited by Hastings Elwin.] 4to, half cloth. Privately printed.

Norwich, 1853.

Only 100 copies printed. "The notes to this play by Mr. Elwin, the most able of any of its critics, which form so distinguishing and important a feature in the present edition are extracted from a privately-printed book, entitled *Shakespeare Restored*, 4to, Norwich, 1853.—*Halliwell's Folio Shakespeare, Note to Macbeth.*

115 Shakespeare's Hamlet. Herausgegeben von Karl Elze. 8vo, new half morocco, red top, uncut. Leipzig, 1857.

The English text, with full commentary in German.

116 The Sonnets of William Shakspere, rearranged and divided into Four Parts. With an Introduction and Explanatory Notes. [By Robert Cartwright.] 12mo, cloth, uncut. London, 1859.

117 The Tempest. By William Shakespeare. Illustrated by Birket Foster, Gustave Dorè, Frederick Skill, Alfred Slader, and Gustave Janet. Small 4to, full morocco, gilt edges. New York, [1860].

A handsome volume. Without Introduction or Notes.

118 The Most Excellent Historie of The Merchant of Venice Written by William Shakspeare. *Illustrated.* Small 4to, full morocco, gilt edges. London, 1860.

Slightly expurgated, "as a Gift-book for Families." Illustrated by Birket Foster and others.

119 Shakespeare's Tempest Edited with Glossarial and Explanatory Notes by the Rev. J. M. Jephson. 16mo, limp cloth. London, 1864.

Textual notes, in pencil, by Mr. Crosby.

120 William Shakespeare's Coriolanus Edited by F. A. Leo Ph. D. With a Quarto-Facsimile of the Tragedy of Coriolanus from the Folio of 1623 Photo-lithographed by A. Burchard and with Extracts from North's Plutarch. Royal 8vo, brown vellum cloth, uncut.

London, 1864.

Printed in Berlin. Apparently, large paper copy. "The notes are critical and masterly, and just what an advanced Shakespeare student requires." *Joseph Crosby.*

121 The Poems of Shakespeare. With a Memoir by Rev.
Alexander Dyce. 16mo, half morocco, gilt tops, uncut.
Boston, 1864.

122 Songs and Sonnets by William Shakespeare. [Edited by
Francis Turner Palgrave. Gem Edition.] 16mo,
cloth, uncut. London and Cambridge, 1865.

123 Shakespeare. With Critical and Explanatory Notes. By
the Rev. John Hunter. 35 vols., 12mo, limp cloth.
London, 1865-73.

124 Shakespeare's Sonnets, with Commentaries, by Thomas
D. Budd. 16mo, original wrappers, uncut. Pp. 172.
Philadelphia, 1868.
The author contends that the person addressed in the Sonnets "is no
other than the soul materialized."

125 The Tragicall Historie of Hamlet, Prince of Denmarke,
by William Shakespeare. Edited according to the first
printed Copies, with the Various Readings, and Critical Notes, by F. H. Stratmann. 8vo, half calf, marbled
edges. London (Krefeld), 1869.
In the old spelling.

126 Shakspere's Hamlet, Prince of Denmark. Englischer
Text, berichtigt und erklärt von Dr. Benno Tschisch-
witz. 12mo, cloth. Halle, 1869.

127 Shakespeare's Midsummer-Night's Dream. The Designs
by P. Konewka. Small 4to, cloth, gilt edges.
Boston, 1870.
Beautiful silhouette.illustrations.

128 Charles Kemble's Shakspere Readings: Being a Selection of the Plays of Shakspere, as read by him in Public. Edited by R. J. Lane. 3 vols., crown 8vo, cloth.
London, 1870.
The pagination is continuous, 932 pp.

129 A new Variorum Edition of Shakespeare Edited by
Horace Howard Furness Vol. I Romeo and Juliet.

8vo, half blue calf gilt, gilt top.　Philadelphia, 1871.

A few manuscript notes by Mr. Crosby in margins and on fly-leaf.
This edition is well denominated "a perfect library of Shakespearian literature in itself." For other volumes, see Nos. 135, 140, 148.

130 Shakespeare. With Notes by Wm. J. Rolfe, A. M. Illustrated.　40 vols., 16mo, red cloth, red edges.

New York, 1871–84.

A complete set of this valuable edition. At least sixteen of the volumes are presentation copies to Mr. Crosby, with the editor's autograph. Some of the volumes contain numerous notes in pencil by Mr. Crosby. A part of the volumes are expurgated, for school and family use.

131 *The same.* Henry VIII. (2 copies), The Tempest.　3 vols.

132 The Songs of Shakspere　Selected from his Poems and Plays. *Chandos Portrait.* 16mo, cloth, gilt edges.

London, 1872.

133 Shakespeare's King Lear with Notes, Examination Papers, and Plan of Preparation. Edited by J. M. D. Meiklejohn. *Also, in the same series,* Merchant of Venice, Tempest, Hamlet, Macbeth, Richard II., Henry V.　7 vols., crown 8vo, cloth.

W. & R. Chambers London and Edinburgh [1872–80].

An excellent school and family edition.

134 Select Plays of Shakspere.　The Rugby Edition.　With an Introduction and Notes to each Play.　Edited by the Rev. Charles E. Moberley, and others. *The Plays are :* As You Like It, Macbeth, Hamlet, King Lear, Romeo and Juliet, Coriolanus, The Tempest, A Midsummer-Night's Dream, King Henry the Fifth.　9 vols., small 8vo, half morocco.

Rivingtons, London, 1872–81.

These plays are ably edited, and are very handy.

135 A New Variorum Edition of Shakespeare Edited by Horace Howard Furness Vol. II Macbeth. 8vo, cloth, uncut.　Philadelphia, 1873.

See No. 129. The plan of the edition is somewhat extended in this volume. "In the present volume will be found, therefore, such notes and comments from all sources as I have deemed worthy of preservation, either for the purpose of elucidating the text, or as illustrations of the history of Shakespearian criticism."—*Author's Preface.* It is unnecessary to add that the execution of this great undertaking has received the universal applause of Shakespearian students.

136 The Second Part of Henry the Fourth . . . . . Arranged for Representation By Charles Calvert. Small 8vo, half cloth. Manchester, 1874.

137 Shakespeare's Songs and Sonnets Illustrated by John Gilbert. The Poets of the Elizabethan Age. A Selection of their most Celebrated Songs and Sonnets. Illustrated with Thirty Engravings. 2 vols., small 8vo, cloth, gilt edges. *The Choice Series.*
London and New York, [1875].

138 Pitt Press Series. Shakespeare and Fletcher. The Two Noble Kinsmen. Edited by the Rev. Walter W. Skeat. Post 8vo, cloth. Cambridge and London, 1875.

139 Collins' School and College Classics. Shakespeare's Tempest, Merchant of Venice, Richard II., Richard III., King Henry VIII., King Lear, Macbeth, As You Like It, Julius Cæsar, Hamlet, Coriolanus, Midsummer Night's Dream, King John, King Henry V., Romeo and Juliet. With Introductory Remarks; Explanatory, Grammatical, and Philological Notes; etc. By Neil, Lawson, Fleay, and others. 15 vols., foolscap 8vo, cloth. London and Glasgow, 1875-79.

140 A New Variorum Edition of Shakespeare Edited by Horace Howard Furness. Vols. III., IV. Hamlet. 2 vols., 8vo, cloth, uncut. Philadelphia, 1877.

See Nos. 129, 135. This copy has a few manuscript notes by Mr. Crosby. Inserted is an interesting autograph letter from the Editor to Mr. Crosby.

141 *The same.* Vol. II., cloth, uncut.
Philadelphia, 1877.

142 Clarendon Press Series Shakespeare Select Plays Edited by William Aldis Wright. A Midsummer Night's Dream, Julius Cæsar, Coriolanus, King Richard the Third, King Henry the Fifth. 5 vols., 12mo, new half morocco. Oxford, 1877-81.

143 Edwin Booth's Prompt-Books. Edited by William Winter. Hamlet, King Richard the Second, King Lear, The Merchant of Venice. 4 vols., 16mo, original paper covers. New York, 1878.

144 Shakespeare's Henry the Fifth. Erklärt von Dr. Wilh. Wagner. 12mo, cloth. Berlin, 1878.
English text, with Introduction and Notes in German.

145 The Hamnet Shakspere. According to The First Folio (spelling modernized). With Introduction and Relative Lists. By Allan Park Paton. Vol. I., containing five Plays, viz. Macbeth, Cymbeline, Hamlet, Timon, Winters Tale. 8vo, half morocco, red top, uncut, contents lettered. Edinburgh and London, 1879-80.
The editor has a peculiar theory in regard to Shakespeare's use of "Emphasis—Capitals." Each play is paged separately.

146 Hudson's Revised and Enlarged Editions of the Shakespeare Plays for School and Family Use. Romeo and Juliet, Cymbeline, Coriolanus, Othello, As You Like It, Hamlet. 6 vols., square 12mo, cloth. Boston, 1879-81.
Two are presentation copies—" Mr. Joseph Crosby. From the Editor."

147 Shakespeare. King Henry the Fifth. With Notes and Introduction. By K. Deighton. Small 8vo, cloth, uncut. London, 1880.

148 A New Variorum Edition of Shakespeare Edited by Horace Howard Furness Vol. V King Lear. 8vo, cloth, uncut. Philadelphia, 1880.
See Nos. 129, 135, 140. The last volume of this great work thus far published. Presentation copy, with autograph letter from the Editor to Mr. Crosby inserted.

149 Shakespeare   Macbeth   Edition Classique, par James
Darmesteter.   12mo, half morocco.   Paris, 1881.
English text, with Introduction and Notes in French.

150 The Shakespeare Reader; being Extracts from the Plays
of Shakespeare . . . . . . With Introductory Para-
graphs and Notes, Grammatical, Historical, and Explanatory. By C. H. Wykes. 16mo, cloth.
New York, 1881.

151 The Sonnets of William Shakspere   Edited by Edward
Dowden.   Foolscap 8vo; parchment, gilt top, uncut.
London, 1881.

152 The Sonnets of William Shakspere   Edited by Edward
Dowden.   [Enlarged Edition.]   Crown 8vo, cloth, uncut.   London, 1881.
    " The present Edition differs from that in the Parchment Series in hav-
ing fuller notes, and Part II. of the Introduction, giving a survey of the
Literature of the Sonnets."—Note by the Author. The best guide to the
study of the Sonnets.

153 Shakespeare for Young Folks.   A Midsummer-Night's
Dream.   As You Like It.   Julius Cæsar.   Edited by
Robert H. Raymond, A. M.   8vo, cloth, gilt edges.
New York, [1881].

154 *Separate Plays of Shakespeare.*   The Globe Edition
reprinted by the American Book Exchange.   18 plays
(3 duplicates), 16mo, paper covers.
New York, 1881–82.

155 Shakespeare's Tragedy of Hamlet   edited by Karl Elze.
8vo, cloth, uncut.   London, 1882.
    An attempt to reproduce the play in Shakespeare's own spelling. The
notes are extensive.

156 The Shakspere Reading Book: being Seventeen of Shakspere's Plays abridged for the use of Schools and Public Readings.   By H. Courthope Bowen.   Crown 8vo,
cloth.   London, [1882].

157 Shakespeare's Plays, with Notes. *Meiklejohn's edition*
(see No. 133) *abridged* by Brainerd Kellogg. Macbeth,
Tempest, King Lear, Julius Cæsar, Hamlet, Merchant
of Venice, King Henry V., As You Like It.   8 vols.,
32mo, cloth, red edges.   New York, 1882–83.

158 Shakspeare's Historical Plays   Roman and English with
Revised text, Introductions, and Notes Glossarial, Critical, and Historical   by Charles Wordsworth. 3 vols.,
crown 8vo, cloth, uncut, new.   London, 1883.

159 Longmans' Modern Series.   Shakespeare's Julius Cæsar
with Introduction, Notes, Examination Papers and an
Appendix of Prefixes and Terminations.   By Thomas
Parry.   Small 8vo, cloth.   London, 1883.

160 English Comic Dramatists   Edited by Oswald Crawfurd.
Foolscap 8vo, parchment, gilt top, uncut.
                                   New York, 1883.
Contains an extract from King Henry IV., Part 1.

161 *Six odd parts of Shakespeare's Works*, each containing
a complete Play.   Paper covers.   London, v. d.

III. SHAKESPEARIANA.

162 Of Dramatick Poesie.   An Essay.   By John Dreyden.
Small 4 to, half morocco.   Foxed.   London, 1684.
Second Edition, revised and enlarged.

163 A Short View of Tragedy; It's Original, Excellency, and
Corruption.   With some Reflections on Shakespear,
and other Practitioners for the Stage.   By Mr. Rymer.
16mo, old calf.   Clean copy.   London, 1693.
Chapter 7, on *Othello*, is a masterpiece of stupidity.   Macaulay characterized Rymer as "the worst critic that ever lived."

3

164 Shakespeare restored; or, a Specimen of the Many Errors,
as well Committed, as Unamended, by Mr. Pope In his
Late Edition of this Poet. Designed not only to correct the said Edition, but to restore the True Reading
of Shakespeare in all the Editions ever yet publish'd.
By Mr. Theobald. 4 to, half russia. Good copy.

London, 1726.

The beginning of the famous Pope-Theobald controversy. Pope was
severely handled, and Theobald was pilloried in The Dunciad. SCARCE.

165 Miscellaneous Observations on the Tragedy of Macbeth;
with Remarks on Sir T. Hanmer's Edition of Shakespeare. First Printed in 1745. [By Dr Samuel Johnson.] Pp. 59-114, of some volume of an early edition
of Johnson's works.

166 Critical Observations on Shakespeare. By John Upton.
8vo, sheep. London, 1746.

Original edition containing 9 pages omitted in later edition.

167 An Attempte To Rescue that Aunciente, English Poet,
and Play-Wrighte, Maister Williaume Skakespere, from
the Maney Errours, faulsely charged on him, by Cer-
taine New-fangled Wittes; and To let him Speak for
Himself, as right well he wotteth, when Freede from
the many Careless Misktakeings, of The Heedless first
Imprinters, of his Workes. By a Gentleman formerly
of Greÿs-Inn [John Holt]. Small 8vo, half morocco. Pp. 94. London, 1749.

Has book-plate of Joseph Parker Norris. A present from him to Mr.
Crosby. RARE.

168 Shakespear Illustrated: or the Novels and Histories, On
which the Plays of Shakespear Are Founded, Collected
and Translated from the Original Authors. With Critical Remarks. By the Author of the Female Quixote
[Mrs. C. Lennox]. 3 vols., small 8vo, old calf.

London, 1753-54.

The dedication is said to have been written by Dr. Johnson. Knight
calls Mrs. Lennox "an average specimen of the insolence of that critical
jargon which looks most like sense."

169 Critical, Historical, and Explanatory Notes on Shakespeare, with Emendations of the Text and Metre, By Zachary Grey, LL. D. 2 vols., full dark leather, red edges. Nice copy. London, 1754.

170 Prolusions; or, select Pieces of antient Poetry,—compil'd with great Care from their several Originals, and offer'd to the Publick as Specimens of the Integrity that should be found in the Editions of worthy Authors,— in three Parts; containing, I. The notbrowne Mayde; Master Sackvile's Induction; and, Overbury's Wife: II. Edward the third, a Play, thought to be writ by Shakespeare: III. Those excellent didactic Poems, intitl'd—*Nosce teipsum*, written by Sir John Davis: with a Preface. [Edited by Edward Capell.] Small 8vo, old calf. London, 1760.
SCARCE.

171 The Canons of Criticism, and Glossary . . . . [By Thomas Edwards.] The Seventh Edition, with Additions. 8vo, half morocco, gilt top, UNCUT. Fine copy.
London, 1765.
Pencil Notes by Mr. Crosby. A popular satire on Warburton. See No. 13.

172 A Revisal of Shakespear's Text, wherein The Alterations introduced into it by the more modern Editors and Critics, are particularly considered. [By Benjamin Heath.] 8vo, sheep, marbled edges. London, 1765.
Numerous notes in pencil by Mr. Crosby. "The great majority of Mr. Heath's notes, conjectures, and emendations, are exceedingly clever and plausible . . . J. C."
"Shows sound wisdom and starts many shrewd conjectures."—*H. H. Furness.*

173 A Review of Dr. Johnson's New Edition of Shakespeare: in which the Ignorance, or Inattention, of that Editor is exposed, and the Poet defended from the Persecution of his Commentators. By W. Kenrick. 8vo, half red morocco. London, 1765.
"A very illiberal and virulent attack."—*Bohn's Lowndes.*

174 The Origin of the English Drama, illustrated in its various Species, viz. Mystery, Morality, Tragedy, and Comedy, by Specimens from our earliest Writers: with Explanatory Notes By Thomas Hawkins. 3 vols., 8vo, tree calf, yellow edges. Oxford, 1773.
   A useful collection.

175 Cursory Remarks on Tragedy, on Shakespear, and on certain French and Italian Poets, principally Tragedians. [By Edward Taylor.] 8vo, new mottled sheep, yellow edges, neat. London, 1774.
   Knight affirms that the author was W. Richardson, Professor of Humanity in the University of Glasgow.

176 The Morality of Shakespeare's Drama Illustrated. By Mrs. Griffith. 8vo, old tree calf, gilt. London, 1775.
   Dedicated to David Garrick.

177 Six Old Plays, on which Shakspeare founded his Measure for Measure. Comedy of Errors. Taming the Shrew. King John. K. Henry IV. and K. Henry V. King Lear. 2 vols in 1, crown 8vo, half calf, rubbed. London, 1779.
   The pagination of the two volumes is continuous. Supplemental to Hawkins's Antient English Dramas (No. 174). Published by J. Nichols, " without departure from the original copies."

178 Memoirs of the Life of David Garrick, Esq . . . . . . By Thomas Davies. 2 vols., 8vo, half green turkey morocco, marbled edges, neat. London, 1780.

179 Remarks, Critical and Illustrative, on the Text and Notes of the Last Edition of Shakspeare. [By Joseph Ritson.] 8vo, full calf, yellow edges, neat. London, 1783.
   Has the rare prospectus leaf at end, and many manuscript notes by Mr. Crosby. SCARCE. Should accompany Johnson and Steevens's Second Edition, 1778. (No. 19.)

180 Dramatic Miscellanies: consisting of Critical Observations on several Plays of Shakespeare: with a Review of his Principal Characters, and those of various emi-

nent Writers, as represented by Mr. Garrick, and other celebrated Comedians. With Anecdotes of Dramatic Poets, Actors, etc. By Thomas Davies. *Portrait of Thomas Betterton.* 3 vols., crown 8vo, new half morocco, red tops, UNCUT. London, 1784.

181 A Catalogue of the Pictures, etc. in the Shakspeare Gallery Pall-Mall. 12mo, half morocco. A leaf gone from the Preface, and one or more at the end.
London, 1790.

182 A Specimen of a Commentary on Shakspeare. Containing I. Notes on As You Like It. II. An Attempt to explain and illustrate Various Passages, on a new principle of Criticism, derived from Mr. Locke's Doctrine of the Association of Ideas. [By the Rev. Walter Whiter.] 8vo, sheep, marbled edges. London, 1794.
Pencil notes by Mr. Crosby. "Superior to the ordinary criticism of that age."—*C. Knight.*

183 Miscellaneous Papers and Legal Instruments under the Hand and Seal of William Shakspeare: including the Tragedy of King Lear, and a small fragment of Hamlet, from the original MSS. in the possession of Samuel Ireland, of Norfolk Street. 8vo, new half morocco, gilt top, UNCUT. London, 1796.

184 A Letter to George Steevens, Esq. containing a Critical Examination of the Papers of Shakspeare; published by Mr. Samuel Ireland. To which are added, Extracts from Vortigern. By James Boaden, Esq. 8vo, half morocco, marbled edges. London, 1796.
First Edition, pp. 72. "This tract first appeared in a newspaper entitled 'The Oracle,' edited by James Boaden."—*Bohn's Lowndes.*

185 A Comparative Review of the Opinions of Mr. James Boaden, (Editor of the Oracle) In February, March, and April, 1795; and of James Boaden, Esq. (Author of Fontainville Forest, and of a Letter to George Steevens, Esq.) In February, 1796, relative to the

Shakspeare MSS. By a Friend to Consistency. Pp. 59.
8vo, half calf, marbled edges.   London, [1796].

186 An Inquiry into the Authenticity of certain Miscellaneous
Papers and Legal Instruments, published Dec. 24,
MDCCXCV. and attributed to Shakspeare, Queen Eliz-
abeth, and Henry, Earl of Southampton: Illustrated
by Fac-similes of the genuine Hand-writing of that
Nobleman and of Her Majesty; a new Fac-simile of the
Hand-writing of Shakspeare, never before exhibited;
and other authentick Documents . . . . By Edmond
Malone, Esq. 8vo, half morocco.   London, 1796.
"The learning and ability displayed by Malone in denouncing Ireland's
most clumsy and palpable of frauds, would have sufficed for the detection of
the most cunningly conceived and skilfully executed."—*The Cambridge Editors.*

187 Shakspeare's Manuscripts, in the Possession of Mr. Ire-
land, Examined, respecting the internal and external
Evidences of their Authenticity. By Philalethes [Col.
F. Webb]. 8vo, cloth. Pp. 34.   London, 1796.

188 An Authentic Account of the Shaksperian Manuscripts,
&c. By W. H. Ireland. 8vo half calf, marbled edges.
Pp. 43.   London: Debrett, 1796.
"The original edition having become very scarce, selling for upwards of
1*l.* 1*s.*, fifty copies were reprinted in imitation of it, by Barker of Russell
Street, which reached the same price."—*Bohn's Lowndes.*

189 Mr. Ireland's Vindication of his Conduct, respecting the
Publication of the Supposed Shakspeare MSS. Being
a Preface or Introduction to A Reply to the Critical
Labors of Mr. Malone, in his "Enquiry into the Authenticity of Certain Papers, &c., &c." 8vo half calf, marbled edges. Pp. 48.   London, 1796.
Published Jan. 2, 1797.

190 An Investigation of Mr. Malone's Claim to the Character
of Scholar, or Critic, Being an Examination of his Inquiry into the Authenticity, of the Shakspeare Manu-

scripts, &c. By Samuel Ireland. 8vo, half calf, marbled edges. Pp. 153. London, [1797].

"From the Author", on title. "Presentation copy, with Ms. note by author (S. Ireland), and an additional page of Addenda not found in published copies."—*Note on fly-leaf, by Mr. Crosby.*

191 Comments on the Plays of Beaumont and Fletcher, with an Appendix, containing some further Observations on Shakespeare, extended to the late Editions of Malone and Steevens. By the Right Honourable J. Monck Mason. 8vo, half morocco, sprinkled edges, neat.

London, 1798.

192 Notes upon some of the Obscure Passages in Shakespeare's Plays; with Remarks upon the Explanations and Amendments of the Commentators in the Editions of 1785, 1790, 1793. By the late Right Hon. John Lord Chedworth. 8vo, half calf, neat. London, 1805.

Edited by T. Penrice, and privately printed. "His Lordship possessed a fine taste and correct scholarship."—*Joseph Crosby.* This copy contains many pencil notes by Mr. Crosby.

193 Remarks, Critical, Conjectural, and Explanatory, upon the Plays of Shakspeare; resulting from a Collation of the Early Copies, with that of Johnson and Steevens, Edited by Isaac Reed, Esq. Together with some valuable Extracts from the MSS. of the late Right Honourable John, Lord Chedworth. Dedicated to Richard Brinsley Sheridan, Esq. By E. H. Seymour. 2 vols., 8vo, half calf, sprinkled edges. London, 1805.

"Seymour was a pedagogue, not a critic."—*R. G. White.*

194 The Pursuits of Literature. A Satirical Poem. 13th Edition, with the Citations translated. [By T. J. Mathias.] 8vo, old marbled calf, yellow edges.

London, 1805.

195 Comments on the Several Editions of Shakespeare's Plays, extended to those of Malone and Steevens. By the

Right Honorable John Monck Mason. 8vo, half morocco, sprinkled edges.   Dublin, 1807.

" 250 copies printed."—*Bohn's Lowndes.* " From Mason I have got more
useful and edifying instruction, than almost any other of the old line commentators."—*Joseph Crosby.* Numerous pencil notes by Mr. Crosby.

196 Comments on the Commentators of Shakespear. With
Preliminary Observations on his Genius and Writings;
and on the Labors of those who have endeavoured to
elucidate them. By Henry James Pye.

London, 1807.

Essays on some of Shakespeare's Dramatic Characters.
To which is added, An Essay on the Faults of Shake-
speare. The Fifth Edition. By William Richardson.
London, 1797.

The 2 in 1 volume, 8vo, half russia, marbled edges.

Notes in pencil by Mr. Crosby. Pye's Observations were made on the
Edition of Nichols, 1797. (See No. 27.)

197 Illustrations of Shakspeare, and of Ancient Manners:
with Dissertations on the Clowns and Fools of Shak-
speare; on the Collection of Popular Tales entitled
Gesta Romanorum; and on the English Morris Dance.
By Francis Douce. The Engravings on wood by J.
Berryman. 2 vols., 8vo, full sprinkled calf.

London, 1807.

The citations are to "Steevens's Own," 1793. (See No. 24.) " The critical
student of Shakespeare can place upon his shelves no book of comments
more valuable than the two volumes of Francis Douce."—*Richard Grant
White,* 1854. VERY SCARCE.

198 Biographia Dramatica; or, a Companion to the Playhouse: containing Historical and critical Memoirs and
original Anecdotes, of British and Irish Dramatic
Writers from the Commencement of our Theatrical
Exhibitions . . . . By Baker, Reed, and Jones. 3
vols. in 2, 8vo, half morocco, red tops, uncut edges.

London, 1812.

Nice copy of the best edition,

199 An Essay on the Character of Henry the Fifth when
Prince of Wales. By Alexander Luders, Esq.

London, 1813.

An attempt to show that Henry was not "the dissolute young prince"
that Shakespeare represents him to have been.

200 Shakspeare's Himself Again: or The Language of the
Poet Asserted: being a full but dispassionate Examen
of the Readings and Interpretations of the several
Editors. The whole comprised in a series of Notes,
sixteen hundred in number . . . . By Andrew Becket.
2 vols., 8vo, full grained calf. London, 1815.

"I can perceive no knowledge, technical or otherwise, that has served
Andrew Becket in any stead."—H. H. Furness.

201 Shakspeare and His Times: including the Biography of
the Poet; Criticisms on his Genius and Writings; a
new Chronology of his Plays; a Disquisition on the
·Object of his Sonnets; and a History of the Manners,
Customs, and Amusements, Superstitions, Poetry, and
Elegant Literature of his Age. By Nathan Drake.
Portrait, after the Stratford Bust. 2 vols., 4to, half
morocco, gilt tops. London, 1817.

"This invaluable storehouse of Shakspearean information."—Allibone.

202 Macbeth, and King Richard the Third: an Essay, in answer to Remarks on some of the Characters of Shakspeare. By J. P. Kemble. Small 8vo, half calf. Foxed.

London, 1817.

In answer to Whately's "Remarks", London, 1785.

203 Illustrations of the Literary History of the Eighteenth
Century. Consisting of Authentic Memoirs and Original Letters of Eminent Persons; and intended as a
sequel to The Literary Anecdotes. By John Nichols,
F. S. A. *Numerous fine portraits and other engravings.* 8 vols., 8vo, new calf, extra, gilt backs and edges,
by RIVIERE. London, 1817–1858.

Some pages of earlier volumes foxed; otherwise, a beautiful copy of this
rare work. Vol. II. (pp. 189–655) contains original letters of Theobald and
Warburton. There are various other references to Shakespeare or his editors throughout the work.

204 The Beauties of Shakspeare, regularly selected from each Play: With a General Index, digesting them under proper heads. By the late Rev. W. Dodd. Foolscap 8vo, new half morocco, gilt edges, neat.

Chiswick: C. Whittingham, 1818.

Contains Britton's Remarks on the Life and Writings of William Shakspeare, and wood-cuts after Thurston's Designs.

205 The Beauties of Shakspeare. By the late W. Dodd. 16mo, diamond calf, marbled edges.

From the Chiswick Press, London, 1818.

In smaller type than the preceding, but beautifully printed.

206 Shakspeare's Genius Justified: being Restorations and Illustrations of Seven Hundred Passages in Shakspeare's Plays: which have afforded abundant scope for critical Animadversion; and hitherto held at defiance the penetration of all Shakspeare's Commentators. By Z. Jackson. 8vo, half morocco, sprinkled edges.

London, 1819.

" Here and there Jackson's technical knowledge of a printer's case has enabled him to make a lucky guess."—*H. H. Furness*. " The very *Bunsby* of commentators."—*R. G. White.*

207 The Poetical Decameron, or Ten Conversations on English Poets and Poetry, particularly of the Reigns of Elizabeth and James I. By J. Payne Collier. 2 vols. in 1, small 8vo, calf, marbled edges.   London, 1820.

208 An Essay on the Dramatic Character of Sir John Falstaff. By Maurice Morgann. 12mo, full leather, neat.

London, 1820.

" The author is a thinker, and one who has been taught to think by Shakspere."—*C. Knight.*

209 An Inquiry into the Authenticity of Various Pictures and Prints, which, from the Decease of the Poet to our own Times, have been offered to the Public as Portraits of Shakspeare: containing a careful Examination of the Evidence on which they claim to be received; by which the Pretended Portraits have been rejected,

the Genuine confirmed and established. Illustrated
by accurate and finished Engravings, by the ablest
Artists, from such Originals as were of indisputable
authority. By James Boaden, Esq. 8vo, new half
morocco, gilt top, UNCUT. London, 1824.
FINE COPY. "To S. W. Singer, Esq., with the Publisher's kind regards."

210 The Life of Shakspeare; Enquiries into the Originality
of his Dramatic Plots and Characters; and Essays on
the Ancient Theatres and Theatrical Usages. By
Augustine Skottowe. 2 vols., 8vo, half morocco, gilt
tops, uncut. London, 1824.
Fine copy. MS. index to each volume, by Mr. Crosby.

211 Dodsley's Old Plays in Twelve Volumes. [Edited by J.
Payne Collier.] Vols. 4 to 12, 9 vols., half morocco,
red edges. London, 1825–27.

212 An Essay on the Genius of Shakespeare, with Critical
Remarks on the Characters of Romeo, Hamlet, Juliet,
and Ophelia; together with some Observations on the
Writings of Sir Walter Scott. . . . . . . By Henry
Mercer Graves. Small 8vo, half morocco, red edges.
London, 1826.
Bound with this is "Studies in Literature," by G. W. Griffin, Baltimore,
1870.

213 An Appendix to Shakspeare's Works . . . . . 8vo, half
calf. Foxed. Leipsic, 1826.
Contents: The Life of the Author by Aug. Skottowe; his Miscellaneous
Poems; A Critical Glossary, etc.

214 An Index to the Remarkable Passages and Words made
use of by Shakspeare; calculated to point cut the different Meanings to which the words are applied. By
the Rev. Samuel Ayscough. 8vo, half morocco, red
edges. London, 1827.

215 Shaksperiana. Catalogue of all the Books, Pamphlets,
&c., relating to Shakspeare. To which are subjoined,

an Account of the Early Quarto Editions of the Great
Dramatist's Plays and Poems. The Prices at which
many Copies have sold in Public Sales; together with
a List of the leading and esteemed Editions of Shakspeare's Collected Works. Small 8vo, cloth, uncut.

London, 1827.

" Still valuable, for the sake of the Preface, which contains an account
of fabricated portraits of Shakspeare."—*Allibone*.

216 *The same.* Original boards, uncut. London, 1827.
"Mr. Joseph Crosby, with the regards of W. H. Wyman. Cincinnati,
March 9, 1881."

217 Supplement to Wivell's Portraits. 8vo, boards, uncut. ·
London, 1827.
Lacks portraits.

218 Memorials of Shakspeare; or, Sketches of his Character
and Genius, by various Writers, now first Collected:
with a Prefatory and Concluding Essay, and Notes, by
Nathan Drake . . . . Forming a valuable Accompani-
ment to every Edition of the Poet. 8vo, full red calf,
marbled edges. London, 1828.
Many scarce papers are here brought together in a compendious form.

219 Shaksperian Anthology : comprising the Choicest Passages and entire Scenes; selected from the most correct Editions; with a Biographical Sketch.

London, 1830.

Shakspeare's Seven Ages of Man; or, the Progress of
Human Life . . . . By John Evans. London, 1834.

The two in one volume, half morocco, red edges.

220 The History of English Dramatic Poetry to the Time of
Shakespeare: and Annals of the Stage to the Restoration. By J. Payne Collier. 3 vols., 8vo, calf, marbled
edges. London, 1831.

221 Vortigern; an Historical Play; with an Original Preface.
· By W. H. Ireland. Represented at Theatre Royal,

' Drury Lane, on Saturday, April 2, 1796, as a supposed newly-discovered Drama of Shakspeare. 8vo, original wrappers. London, 1832.

222 The Spirit of the Plays of Shakspeare, exhibited in a Series of Outline Plates illustrative of the Story of each Play. Drawn and engraved by Frank Howard. With Quotations and Descriptions. *483 plates and 1 portrait, India proofs,* mounted with letterpress on large paper, in 10 cloth cases. Some plates slightly foxed. 10 vols., folio. London, 1833.

223 A letter on Shakspeare's Authorship of The Two Noble Kinsmen ; a Drama commonly ascribed to John Fletcher. [By W. Spalding.] 8vo, cloth, uncut. London, 1833.
Fine copy, on ribbed paper. Has book-plate of John Adolphus Esqre.

224 Citation and Examination of William Shakspeare Euseby Treen Joseph Carnaby and Silas Gough Clerk before the Worshipful Sir Thomas Lucy Knight touching Deer-stealing On the 19th day of September in the year of Grace 1582 Now first published from Original Papers .... [By Walter Savage Landor.] 12mo, new half morocco, uncut. London, 1834.
Clean copy of the First Edition.

225 Life of Mrs. Siddons. By Thomas Campbell. 2 vols., 8vo, half calf gilt, marbled edges. London, 1834.
Nice copy of the First Edition.

226 New Facts regarding the Life of Shakespeare. In a Letter to Thomas Amyot, Esq. .... from J. Payne Collier, F. S. A. London, 1835.

New Particulars regarding the Works of Shakespeare. In a Letter to the Rev. A. Dyce, ... from J. Payne Collier, F. S. A. London, 1836.
2 vols. in 1, full calf.
A very small number of each privately printed.

227 The Literary Remains of Samuel Taylor Coleridge Collected and Edited by Henry Nelson Coleridge. 4 vols., 8vo, full calf.
London William Pickering 1836–9.
SCARCE. The Second Volume is largely composed of the well-known lectures on Shakespeare.

228 Shakespeare's Autobiographical Poems. Being his Sonnets clearly Developed : with his Character drawn chiefly from his Works. By Charles Armitage Brown. 8vo, cloth, uncut.   London, 1838.

229 Observations on an Autograph of Shakspere, and the Orthography of his Name. Communicated to the Society of Antiquaries by Sir Frederic Madden. . . . 8vo, original wrappers, pp. 16.   London, 1838.

230 Traditionary Anecdotes of Shakespeare. Collected in Warwickshire, in the year MDCXCIII. Now first published from the Original Manuscript. 8vo, original wrappers, pp. 20.   London, 1838.
Edited by J. Payne Collier (?).

231 The Wisdom and Genius of Shakspeare; comprising Moral Philosophy—Delineations of Character—Paintings of Nature and the Passions—Seven Hundred Aphorisms—and Miscellaneous Pieces. . . . . By the Rev. Thomas Price. Small 8vo, half morocco, marbled edges, neat.   London, 1838.

232 Illustrations of Shakspeare, and of Ancient Manners: with Dissertations on the Clowns and Fools of Shakspeare; on the Collection of Popular Tales entitled Gesta Romanorum; and on the English Morris Dance. By Francis Douce. The Engravings on Wood by Jackson. A New Edition. 8vo, new half morocco, gilt top.   London, 1839.
Marginal notes, by Mr. Crosby. See No. 197.

233 Shakspearian Readings: selected and adapted for Young Persons and Others. By B. H. Smart. First Series,

Illustrative of English and Roman History. 12mo, full leather, gilt, marbled edges, neat. London, 1839.

234 Remarks on some of the Characters of Shakespere, by Thomas Whately, Esq. Edited by Richard Whately, D. D., Archbishop of Dublin. The Third Edition. 16mo, cloth, uncut. London, 1839.

On Richard III. and Macbeth—a parallel. Marginal notes by Mr. Crosby.

235 Diary of the Rev. John Ward, A. M., Vicar of Stratford-upon-Avon, extending from 1648 to 1679. From the Original MSS. preserved in the Library of the Medical Society of London. Arranged by Charles Severn, M. D. 8vo, half green morocco, marbled edges, neat. London, 1839.

Several references to Shakespeare at pp. 183, 184. A large part of the introduction (pp. 29-87) is taken up with an account of Shakespeare.

236 Commentaries on the Historical Plays of Shakspeare. By the Right Hon. Thomas Peregrine Courtenay. 2 vols. in 1, 12mo, half calf, gilt top. London, 1840.

Largely reprinted from The New Monthly Magazine.

237 Kemps Nine Daies Wonder: performed in a Daunce from London to Norwich. With an Introduction and Notes by the Rev. Alexander Dyce. Small 4to, original cloth. London: Camden Society, 1840.

First printed in 1600. Kemp was a comic actor and took the part of Dogberry when Much Ado was first brought out.

238 The Seven Ages of Shakspeare. *Twelve Illustrations.* 4to, half red morocco. London, 1840.

Bound with this are "The Seven Ages," etched by Goodall, London, 1850; and "Shakspere's Seven Ages of Life," illustrated by John Gilbert, Engraved by Thomas Gilks. Second Edition, London, n. d.

239 An Introduction to Shakespeare's Midsummer Night's Dream. By James Orchard Halliwell, Esq. 8vo, half morocco, uncut. London William Pickering 1841.

Has book-plate of Joseph Parker Norris.

240 Shakesperiana. A Catalogue of the Early Editions of Shakespeare's Plays, and of the Commentaries and

other Publications Illustrative of his Works. By
James Orchard Halliwell. 8vo, original cloth.

London, 1841.

Additions in pencil by Mr. Crosby.

241 On the Character of Sir John Falstaff, as originally exhibited by Shakespeare in the Two Parts of King
Henry IV. By James Orchard Halliwell. Small 8vo,
original cloth, uncut. London, 1841.

242 PUBLICATIONS OF THE SHAKESPEARE SOCIETY. 48 volumes, original cloth, uncut. London, 1841–53.
Fresh, clean copy of this important set of publications. Some of the
volumes have become very searce.

243 Reasons for a New Edition of Shakespeare's Works,
containing Notices of the Defects of Former Impres-
sions, and pointing out the lately acquired Means of
Illustrating the Plays, Poems, and Biography of the
Poet. By J. Payne Collier. Second Edition, with
Additions. 8vo, original wrappers. London, 1842.

244 Shakespeare's Library: a Collection of the Romances,
Novels, Poems, and Histories used by Shakespeare as
the Foundation of his Dramas. Now first collected,
and accurately reprinted from the original Editions.
With Introductory Notices, by J. Payne Collier, Esq.
F. S. A. 2 vols., 8vo, new half red morocco, gilt tops,
uncut. Nice copy. London, [1843].

245 An Account of the only known Manuscript of Shakespeare's Plays, comprising some important Variations
and Corrections in the Merry Wives of Windsor,
obtained from a Playhouse copy of that Play recently
discovered. By James Orchard Halliwell, Esq. 8vo,
original wrappers, 24 pp. London, 1843.

246 Remarks on Mr. J. P. Collier's and Mr. C. Knight's
Editions of Shakespeare. By the Rev. Alexander
Dyce. 8vo, half morocco, gilt top, uncut.

London, 1844.

Many marginal notes, throughout, by Mr. Crosby.

247 Richard III. As Duke of Gloucester and King of England. .By Caroline A. Halsted. 2 vols., 8vo, half red morocco, gilt top, uncut. London, 1844.

Vol. I. contains a chapter on "The Character of Richard Duke of Gloucester considered with reference to Shakespeare's Tragedy of Richard III." Pp. 268-296.

248 New Illustrations of the Life, Studies, and Writings of Shakespeare. Supplementary to all the Editions. By Joseph Hunter. 2 vols., 8vo, half red morocco, gilt tops, uncut. London, 1845.

Many notes in pencil by Mr. Crosby. "A judicious, careful, and agreeable critic."—*Joseph Crosby.*

249 Who was "Jack Wilson," the Singer of Shakespeare's Stage? An attempt to prove the Identity of this person with John Wilson, Doctor of Musick, in the University of Oxford, A. D. 1644. By Edward F. Rimbault. 8vo, original wrappers, 16 pp. London, 1846.

250 Shakspeare's Dramatic Art; and his Relation to Calderon and Goethe. Translated from the German of Dr. Hermann Ulrici. 8vo, half morocco, gilt top, uncut.
London, 1846.

251 Criticism Applied to Shakspere. A Series of Essays published originally in the Surplice. By Charles Badham. 12mo, original wrappers. London, 1846.

Many marginal notes by Mr. Crosby.

252 Shakspeare Novels. The Youth of Shakspeare. Shakspeare and his Friends. The Secret Passion. [By Robert Folkestone Williams.] The three in 1 vol., half sheep, rubbed. New York, 1847.

The Author of these interesting tales was a Professor of History, at Richmond. England, and for a time was editor of The New Monthly Magazine.

253 Studies of Shakespeare in the Plays of King John, Cymbeline, Macbeth, As You Like It, Much Ado About Nothing, Romeo and Juliet: with Observations on the

4

Criticism and Acting of those Plays. By George Fletcher. 8vo, half red morocco, gilt top, uncut.

London, 1847.

<small>Reprinted with slight alterations and additions from "The Athenæum" and "The Westminster Review."</small>

254 Shakespeare Proverbs; or, the Wise Saws of our Wisest Poet collected into a Modern Instance. By Mary Cowden Clarke. 16mo, limp cloth, gilt edges.

London, 1848.

255 An Inquiry into the Philosophy and Religion of Shakspere. By W. J. Birch. 8vo, new half morocco, red tops. London, 1848.

<small>An attempt to show that Shakespeare was an athiest.</small>

256 The Life of William Shakespeare. Including many Particulars respecting the Poet and his Family never before published. By James Orchard Halliwell, Esq. 8vo, new half morocco, red top, uncut. London, 1848.

257 Lectures on Shakspeare. By H. N. Hudson. 2 vols, 12mo, half morocco, red edges. New York, 1848.

258 Gallery to Shakspeare's Dramatic Works. In Outlines Invented and Engraved by Moritz Retzsch. Complete in one Volume. With Explanations. Oblong folio, strongly bound in half morocco.

New York (Leipzig), 1849.

<small>First American Original Edition. Authorized by Ernest Fleischer in Leipzig. The German plates, with change of title-page.</small>

259 Studies of Shakspere: forming a Companion Volume to every Edition of the Text. By Charles Knight. 8vo, half morocco, gilt top, uncut. London, 1849.

<small>A republication, with additions and corrections, of the critical Notices scattered through the Pictorial and Library editions by the same author. See Nos. 50, 52.</small>

260 Prize Essay on the Historical Plays of Shakspeare. Written for the Stephen Endowment Prize, King's College, London. [By Thomas Macknight.] 12mo, half calf, marbled edges. London, 1850.

261 The Girlhood of Shakespeare's Heroines; in a Series of Fifteen Tales. By Mary Cowden Clarke. 3 vols., small 8vo, red cloth, gilt edges. London, [1850-52].

262 Lectures and Essays. By Henry Giles. 2 vols., 12mo, cloth. Boston, 1851.
    Volume 1. (pp. 1-44) contains a lecture on " Falstaff. A Type of Epicurean Life."

263 Essays and Marginalia. By Hartley Coleridge. Edited by his Brother. *Portrait.* 2 vols., post 8vo, half morocco, marbled edges. London, 1851.
    SCARCE. Contains considerable Shakespearian matter.

264 Three Essays on Shakespeare's Tragedy of King Lear. By Pupils of the City of London School. 8vo.
    London, 1851.
    The first of these essays is a Parallel between " King Lear " and "Œdipus in Colono," by J. R. Seeley, since distinguished as a writer and critic.

265 Shakspeare and his Times. By M. Guizot. 8vo, half green morocco, marbled edges. London, 1852.

266 A Few Remarks on the Emendation, "Who smothers her with Painting," in the Play of Cymbeline. Discovered by Mr. Collier, in a Corrected Copy of the Second Edition of Shakespeare. By J. O. Halliwell, Esq. 15 pp. 8vo, original wrappers. London, 1852.

267 Shakspere: His Times and Contemporaries. By George Tweddell. 16mo, cloth. London, 1852.

268 Shakespeare's Puck, and his Folklore, illustrated from the Superstitions of all Nations, but more especially from the Earliest Religion and Rites of Northern Europe and the Wends. By William Bell. 3 vols., 12mo, cloth. London, 1852-[64].
    The author argues that Shakespeare spent some time in Germany and the Low Countries during his early life.

269 A Few Notes on Shakespeare; with occasional Remarks on the Emendations of the Manuscript-Corrector in Mr.

Collier's Copy of the Folio 1632. By the Rev. Alexander Dyce. 8vo, half red morocco, gilt top, uncut.
London, 1853.

Many pencil notes by Mr. Crosby, which the binder has cut into in some
places.

270 The Text of Shakespeare Vindicated from the Interpolations and Corruptions advocated by John Payne Collier Esq. in his Notes and Emendations. By Samuel
Weller Singer. 8vo, half green morocco, gilt top,
uncut. London William Pickering 1853.

Numerous manuscript notes by Mr. Crosby throughout. "This was the
first publication against the genuineness of the Perkins Manuscript."—
Bohn's Lowndes. The controversy, in which various distinguished critics
took a hand, was continued for several years, and rivalled in bitterness the
Pope-Theobald and Steevens-Malone controversies of the last century.

271 The Grimaldi Shakspere. Notes and Emendations on
the Plays of Shakspere, from a recently-discovered
Annotated Copy by the late Joseph Grimaldi, Esq.,
Comedian. . . . . 16 pp. 8vo, half morocco, gilt top,
uncut. London, 1853.

Fine copy of this scarce tract. "A Squib on Mr. Collier's discovery of
the annotated Shakespeare of 1632."—*Bohn's Lowndes.*

272 Curiosities of Modern Shaksperian Criticism. By J. O.
Halliwell, Esq. 32 pp. 8vo, original wrappers.
London, 1853.

"From the Author. 5 August, 1853." A rejoinder to the *Athenæum*
reviewers.

273 A Few Words in Reply to the Animadversions of the
Reverend Mr. Dyce on Mr. Hunter's "Disquisition on
The Tempest" (1839); and his New Illustrations of
the Life, Studies and Writings of Shakespeare (1845)
. . . . . By the Author of the Disquisition and the
Illustrations [Joseph Hunter]. 23 pp. 8vo, paper
covers. London, 1853.

Many notes in pencil by Mr. Crosby. See No. 248.

274 Specimens of English Dramatic Poets who lived about
the Time of Shakspeare. With Notes. By Charles

Lamb. A New Edition, including The Extracts from the Garrick Plays. Crown 8vo, half russia, red edges.

London: Bohn, 1854.

275 Biographical Essays. By Thomas De Quincey. Small 8vo, cloth. Boston, 1854.

The essay on " Shakspeare " occupies pp. 9-100.

276 Shakespeare's Versification and its apparent Irregularities explained by Examples from Early and Late English Writers. By William Sidney Walker. Small 8vo, cloth, uncut. London, 1854.

277 Shakespeare's Scholar: being Historical and Critical Studies of his Text, Characters, and Commentators, with an Examination of Mr. Collier's Folio of 1632. By Richard Grant White, A. M. 8vo, half morocco, gilt top, uncut. New York, 1854.

SCARCE. Chiefly devoted to an examination of Collier's " Old Corrector." Numerous marginal notes by Mr. Crosby.

278 Lectures on English Literature from Chaucer to Tennyson. By Henry Reed. *Portrait*. Small 8vo, half morocco, red edges. Philadelphia, 1855.

279 Lectures on English History and Tragic Poetry, as illustrated by Shakspeare. By Henry Reed. Small 8vo, half morocco, red edges. Title in manuscript.

Philadelphia, 1855.

280 Literary Cookery with reference to Matter attributed to Coleridge and Shakespeare. A Letter addressed to " The Athenæum." With a Postscript, containing some Remarks upon the refusal of that Journal to print it. [By A. E. Brae.] London, 1855.

Collier, Coleridge, and Shakespeare. A Review. By the Author of "Literary Cookery." London, 1860.

The two bound together with other papers by the same author in 1 stout volume. 8vo, half morocco, marbled edges. Nearly a complete set of the author's published papers.

The first of these pamphlets is EXTREMELY SCARCE, the publisher having suppressed it "after selling 20 copies." Mr. Collier prosecuted the publisher for libel, but lost his case.

281 Cambridge Essays, contributed by Members of the University, 1856. 8vo, half russia, red edges.

London, [1856].

Contains a paper (pp. 261-91) on "The Text of Shakespeare," by Charles Badham, D. D.

282 Seven Lectures on Shakespeare and Milton. By the late S. T. Coleridge. A List of all the MS. Emendations in Mr. Collier's Folio, 1632; and an Introductory Preface by J. Payne Collier, Esq. 8vo, full calf, marbled edges. London, 1856.

283 A Letter to M. Regnier, of the Théâtre Français, By George Sand, upon her adaptation to the French Stage of Shakespeare's "As You Like It." Translated by Theodosia Lady Monson. Pp. 24, 8vo, original wrappers. London, 1856.

284 Essays Biographical and Critical: chiefly on English Poets. By David Masson, A. M. 8vo, half morocco, gilt top, uncut. Cambridge, 1856.

Scarce. Contains a paper on "Shakespeare and Goethe," pp. 1-36.

285 The Shakespeare Papers of the late William Maginn, LL. D. Annotated by Dr. Shelton Mackenzie. 12mo, half red morocco, red edges. New York, 1856.

Bound with this is Masson's "British Novelists and their Styles," Cambridge, 1859.

286 Cursory Notes on Various Passages in the Text of Beaumont and Fletcher, as edited by the Rev. Alexander Dyce; and on his "Few Notes on Shakespeare." The Author John Mitford. 8vo, original wrappers.

London, 1856.

287 Shakspere's England; or Sketches of our Social History in the Reign of Elizabeth. By G. W. Thornbury. 2 vols., 8vo, half calf. London, 1856.

288 Hamlet. An Attempt to Ascertain whether the Queen were an Accessory, before the Fact, in the Murder of her first Husband. Pp. 48, 8vo, original wrappers.
London, 1856.

289 The Philosophy of the Plays of Shakespeare Unfolded. By Delia Bacon. With a Preface by Nathaniel Hawthorne. 8vo, fresh cloth, uncut. London, 1857.
" Touchstone is not more circumstantial or more logical than Miss Bacon. .... Mr. Hawthorne, as every reader of ' The Scarlet Letter ' knows, is a humourist of peculiar kind; but his concluding paragraph of introduction to this wild and silly book crowns the list of his drolleries."—*The Athenæum*.

290 Remarks on the Differences in Shakespeare's Versification in different Periods of his Life, and on the like Points of Difference in Poetry generally. [By C. Bathurst.] Post 8vo, half morocco, red edges. London, 1857.
Bound with this is "The Poems of William Shakspeare. Edited by Robert Bell. London, 1855."

291 Bacon and Shakespeare. An Inquiry touching Players, Play-houses, and Play-Writers in the Days of Elizabeth. By William Henry Smith, Esq. To which is appended an Abstract of a MS. respecting Tobie Matthew. Post 8vo, cloth, uncut. London, 1857.
An attempt to prove that Bacon was the author of Shakespeare's Plays.

292 William Shakespeare not an Impostor. By an English Critic [G. H. Townsend]. Post 8vo, cloth.
London, 1857.
An answer to the preceding. "This book comes over us with a cloud of special perplexity,—as a book might do, the object of which was to prove that all men and women really die,—or bearing the title " England no Promontory, but an Island."—*The Athenæum*.

293 Pericles Prince of Tyre. A Novel by George Wilkins, printed in 1608, and founded upon Shakespeare's Play. Edited by Professor Tycho Mommsen. . . . . *Fac-simile*. 8vo, half morocco, red top, uncut. Oldenburg, 1857.

294 Characteristics of Women. Moral, Poetical, and Historical. With Illustrations from the Author's Designs. By Mrs. Jameson. New Edition. 2 vols., 8vo, full violet calf, gilt, marbled edges. Beautiful copy.
London, 1858.

295 Strictures on Mr. Collier's New Edition of Shakespeare, 1858. By the Rev. Alexander Dyce. 8vo, half red morocco, gilt top. London, 1859.
A sharp rejoinder. Many textual notes, in pencil, by Mr. Crosby.

296 Shakespeare's Legal Acquirements Considered. By John Lord Campbell. In a Letter to J. Payne Collier. 12mo, cloth. New York, 1859.

297 A Glossary; or, Collection of Words, Phrases, Names, and Allusions to Customs, Proverbs, etc., which have been thought to require illustration, in the Works of English Authors, particularly Shakespeare and his Contemporaries. By Robert Nares. A New Edition, with considerable additions both of words and examples, by James O. Halliwell and Thomas Wright. 2 vols., 8vo, half morocco, marbled edges. London, 1859.

298 The Shakspeare Fabrications, or, the MS. Notes of the Perkins Folio shown to be of recent Origin. With an Appendix on the Authorship of the Ireland Forgeries. By C. Mansfield Ingleby, Esq. Post 8vo, cloth, uncut.
London, 1859.

299 Collier, Coleridge, and Shakespeare. A Review. By the Author of "Literary Cookery" [A. E. Brae]. 8vo, limp cloth. London, 1860.

300 The same. Limp cloth. London, 1860.

301 The same. Limp cloth. London, 1860.

302 The Medical Knowledge of Shakespeare. By John Charles Bucknill, M. D. 8vo, cloth, uncut.
London, 1860.

303 An Inquiry into the Genuineness of the Manuscript Corrections in Mr. J. Payne Collier's Annotated Shakspere, Folio, 1632 ; and of certain Shaksperian Documents likewise published by Mr. Collier. By N. E. S. A. Hamilton. 8vo, cloth, uncut. London, 1860.

304 Mr. J. Payne Collier's Reply to Mr. N. E. S. A. Hamilton's " Inquiry " into the Imputed Shakespeare Forgeries. 72 pp. 8vo, original wrappers. London, 1860.

305 Strictures on Mr. N. E. S. A. Hamilton's Inquiry into the Genuineness of the MS. Corrections in Mr. J. Payne Collier's Annotated Shakespeare, Folio, 1632. By Scrutator [Charles Rivington]. 28 pp. 8vo, original wrappers. London, 1860.

306 A Review of the Present State of the Shakespearian Controversy. By Thomas Duffy Hardy. 75 pp. 8vo, original wrappers. London, 1860.
"Withdrawn from sale." This is a presentation copy—" E. Hawkins, Esq. from the Author." SCARCE.

307 Shakespeare and the Bible: Showing how much the Great Dramatist was indebted to Holy Writ for his profound Knowledge of Human Nature. By Rev. T. R. Eaton. Third Thousand. Small 8vo, half morocco, red edges.   .   London, [1860].
Bound with this is "Remarks on the Sonnets of Shakespeare" [Hitchcock]. New York, 1866.

308 The Fairy Mythology, illustrative of the Romance and Superstition of various Countries; by Thomas Keightley. A New Edition, Revised and greatly Enlarged. Crown 8vo, half russia, gilt, brown edges.
London: Bohn, 1860.

309 Life of Edmond Malone, Editor of Shakspeare. With Selections from his Manuscript Anecdotes. By Sir James Prior. *Portrait.* 8vo, cloth, gilt edges.
London, 1860.

310 A Critical Examination of the Text of Shakespeare, with
Remarks on his Language and that of his Contemporaries, together with Notes on his Plays and Poems.
By William Sidney Walker. 3 vols., small 8vo, cloth,
uncut.· London, 1860.

Manuscript notes by Mr. Crosby. An important work on textual criticism. "In preparing this [Second] edition I have been greatly assisted by
the late Sidney Walker's *Shakespeare's Versification*, &c. [See No. 276],
and his *Critical Examination*, &c.,——works which undoubtedly form
altogether the most valuable body of verbal criticism on our poet that has
yet appeared from the pen of an individual."—*Alexander Dyce*.

311 The Complete Concordance to Shakspere: being a Verbal
Index to all the Passages in the Dramatic Works of
the Poet. (New and Revised Edition.) By Mrs.
Cowden Clarke. Royal 8vo, half red morocco, gilt
top, uncut. Boston (London), 1860.

312 The Mind of Shakspeare, as· Exhibited in his Works.
By the· Rev. Aaron Augustus Morgan. Second Edition. Small 8vo, cloth, uncut. London, 1861.

313 A Complete View of the Shakspere Controversy, con-
cerning the Authenticity and Genuineness of Manu-
script Matter affecting the Works and Biography of
Shakspere, published by Mr. J. Payne Collier as the
Fruits of his Researches. By C. M. Ingleby, LL. D.
Fac-similes. 8vo, cloth, uncut. London, 1861.

A few pencil notes in the margins by Mr. Crosby.

314 A Course of Lectures on Dramatic Literature, by Augustus William Schlegel. Translated By John Black,
Esq. Revised according to the last German Edition,
by the Rev. A. J. W. Morrison. Crown 8vo, half
russia, brown edges. London, 1861.

Appeared originally in Germany in 1817. "The first definite attempt at
comprehensive aesthetical criticism of Shakspere."—*A. W. Ward*.

315 Shakspere: his Birthplace and its Neighbourhood. By
John R. Wise. Illustrated by W. J. Linton. Crown
8vo, cloth, gilt edges. London, 1861.

Contains a "Glossary of Words still used in Warwickshire to be found in
Shakspere."

316 Bible Truths with Shakspearean Parallels being Selections from Scripture, Moral, Doctrinal, and Preceptial, with Passages illustrative of the Text, from the Writings of Shakspeare. [By James Brown.] Post 8vo, cloth, uncut.   London, 1862.

317 On the Received Text of Shakespeare's Dramatic Writings and its Improvement. By Samuel Bailey. 2 vols., 8vo, half morocco, red tops.   London, 1862-66.
Some pencil notes in margins by Mr. Crosby.

318 Our Old Home. By Nathaniel Hawthorne. 12mo, cloth.
Boston, 1863.
First Edition. Contains a chapter entitled "Recollections of a Gifted Woman" [Miss Delia Bacon]. See No. 289.

319 Shakespere's Home at New Place, Stratford-upon-Avon. Being a History of the "Great House" built in the Reign of King Henry VII., by Sir Hugh Clopton, Knight, and subsequently the property of William Shakespere, Gent., wherein he lived and died. By J. C. M. Bellew. Crown 8vo, cloth, uncut.
London, 1863.

320 Shakespeare-Characters; chiefly those Subordinate. By Charles Cowden Clarke. *Portrait, after the Stratford Bust.* 8vo, cloth, uncut.   London, 1863.
Inserted is a leaf from the author's manuscript of the work.

321 A Study of Hamlet. By John Conolly, M. D. Post 8vo, cloth, uncut.   London, 1863.
"Of all the numerous 'Studies' of Hamlet, this is one of the best."— *Joseph Crosby.*

322 Shakespeare Commentaries by Dr. G. G. Gervinus. Translated under the Author's Superintendence by F. E. Bunnett. 2 vols., 8vo, full tree calf, gilt, marbled edges, by *Jenkins.* Beautiful copy.   London, 1863.
"His criticism is essentially of the historical kind, and directs itself to the moral rather than the aesthetical aspects of his subject. .... May perhaps be called the best history of the poet's genius extant."—*A. W. Ward.*

323 Notes, Criticisms, and Correspondence upon Shakespeare's Plays and Actors. By James Henry Hackett. *Portrait.* 12mo, cloth. New York, 1863.

324 An Historical Account of the Birth-Place of Shakespeare. By the late R. B. Wheler, Esq. Reprinted from the Edition of 1824, with a few Prefatory Remarks by J. O. Halliwell, Esq. 24 pp. 8vo, original wrappers. Stratford-on-Avon, 1863.

325 Life Portraits of William Shakspeare: a History of the various Representations of the Poet, with an examination into their Authenticity. By J. Hain Friswell. Illustrated by Photographs of the most authentic Portraits, and with Views, &c. by Cundall, Downes & Co. 8vo, cloth, gilt edges. London, 1864.
An important work on this subject. Scarce.

326 An Historical Account of the New Place, Stratford-upon-Avon, the Last Residence of Shakespeare. By James O. Halliwell, Esq. *Many Illustrations.* Folio, cloth, uncut, new. London, 1864.
"A worthy supplement to the author's great edition of Shakespeare."

327 Shakespeare Jest-Books; Reprints of the Early and very Rare Jest-Books supposed to have been used by Shakespeare. Edited, with Introduction and Notes, by W. Carew Hazlitt. 3 vols., crown 8vo, half roxburghe, uncut, new. London, 1864.

328 Shakespeare and Stratford-upon-Avon, a "Chronicle of the Time": comprising the salient Facts and Traditions, Biographical, Topographical, and Historical, connected with the Poet and his Birth-Place; together with a full Record of the Tercentenary Celebration. By Robert E. Hunter. *Illustrations.* Small 8vo, cloth, gilt edges. London, 1864.

329 Shakespere: his Birthplace, Home, and Grave. A Pilgrimage to Stratford-on-Avon in the Autumn of 1863.

By the Rev. J. M. Jephson. With Photographic Illustrations by Ernest Edwards. . . . 4to, cloth, gilt edges,
London, 1864.

330 The Life and Genius of Shakespeare. By Thomas Kenney. *Portrait, from the Stratford Bust.* 8vo, cloth, uncut. London, 1864.

331 The Seven Ages of Man described by William Shakespeare Depicted by Robert Smirke. *9 photographs.* Oblong 12mo, limp cloth. London, 1864.

332 On Shakspeare's Knowledge and Use of the Bible. By Charles Wordsworth, D. C. L. Bishop of St. Andrews. Second Edition, Enlarged. Crown 8vo, half morocco, full gilt edges. London, 1864.

333 All About Shakespeare Profusely Illustrated with Wood Engravings by Thomas Gilks, drawn by H. Fitzcook. In Commemoration of the Ter-centenary. *Portraits.* 12mo, original wrappers. London, [1864].

334 The Official Programme of The Tercentenary Festival of the Birth of Shakespeare, To be held at Stratford-upon-Avon, Commencing on Saturday, April 23, 1864. . . . . 94 pp. 8vo, paper covers. London, 1864.

335 Shakspeare Memorial. *Four colored illustrations, and numerous engravings of portraits, views, etc.* Folio, cloth. S. O. Beeton, [London, 1864].

336 *Another copy. One colored illustration.* Folio, limp cloth. [London, 1864.]

337 Chambers's Journal Shakspeare Tercentenary Number. April 23, 1864. Extra Double Number. 8vo.
[Edinburgh, 1864.]

338 Reprints of Scarce Pieces of Shakespeare Criticism No. 1. Remarks on Hamlet, 1736. 52 pp. 12mo, paper covers. London, 1864.
Attributed to Sir Thomas Hanmer. "Its contents are characterized by a genuine appreciation of that noble tragedy."—*J. Parker Norris.*

339 The Tercentenary; or the Three Hundredth Birthday of
William Shakespeare. By Messrs. E. Moses and Son.
29 pp. 8vo, paper covers. London, 1864.
" An advertisement of a tailor's establishment."

340 Tales from Shakspere. By Charles and Mary Lamb.
With Scenes illustrating each Tale. Edited by Charles
Knight. *Numerous Illustrations.* Small 8vo, cloth.
London, [1865?].

341 Shakespeare in Germany in the Sixteenth and Seven-
teenth Centuries: an Account of English Actors in
Germany and the Netherlands and of the Plays performed by them during the same period. By Albert
Cohn. With Two Plates of Facsimiles. 4to, half
morocco, uncut. London, 1865.

342 Shakspere His Inner Life as intimated in his Works
By John A. Heraud. *Portrait.* Thick 8vo, cloth,
uncut. London, 1865.

343 England as seen by Foreigners in the Days of Elizabeth
and James the First. Comprising Translations of the
Journals of the two Dukes of Wirtemberg in 1592 and
1610; both illustrative of Shakespeare. With Extracts
from the Travels of Foreign Princes and others,
copious Notes, an Introduction, and Etchings. By
William Brenchley Rye. 4to, half morocco, red top,
uncut. London, 1865.

344 Shakspeariana from 1564 to 1864. An Account of the
Shakspearian Literature of England, Germany and
France during Three Centuries, with Bibliographical
Introductions by Franz Thimm. 8vo, half vellum, by
PRATT. Interleaved. London, 1865.
Numerous manuscript additions by Mr. Crosby.

345 Three Notelets on Shakespeare. I. Shakespeare in Germany. II. The Folk-Lore of Shakespeare. III. Was

Shakespeare ever a Soldier? By William J. Thoms,
F. S. A. Small 8vo, cloth, uncut. London, 1865.

" Not the least of Mr. Thoms's many services to English literature is the
invention of that admirable word *folk-lore*, which appeared for the first
time in these columns only a few years ago, and has already become a
domestic term in every corner of the world. His illustration of Shakspeare's
knowledge of this little world of fairy dreams and legends is a perfect bit of
criticism."—*The Athenæum*, Dec. 31, 1864.

346 William Shakespeare. By His Eminence Cardinal Wise-
man. 8vo, cloth, uncut. London, 1865.

The last work of this eminent prelate —published posthumously.

347 Shakespeare's Medical Knowledge. By Charles W.
Stearns, M. D. 78 pp. 12mo, paper covers.

New York, 1865.

348 Stray Notes on the Text of Shakespeare, by Henry
Wellesley, D. D. 34 pp. 4to, original wrappers.

London, 1865.

Notes in pencil by Mr. Crosby.

349 Shakespeare's Editors and Commentators. By the Rev.
W. R. Arrowsmith. 52 pp. 8vo, original wrappers.

London, 1865.

" I heard Mr. Dyce repeatedly say that he had never seen so forcibly
stated, or supported by better examples, what he believed to be the only
safe rule of guidance in settling disputed readings."—*John Forster*. Many
notes in pencil by Mr. Crosby.

350 New Readings in Shakspere; or, Proposed Emendations
of the Text. By Robert Cartwright, M. D. 39 pp.
8vo, original wrappers. London, 1866.

Numerous manuscript notes by Mr. Crosby. " These New Readings are
the product of pleasant evenings over Mr. Dyce's Second Edition of Shakspere."—*Preface.*

351 Shakspeare's Delineations of Insanity, Imbecility, and
Suicide. By A. O. Kellogg, M. D. Small 8vo, cloth,
uncut. New York, 1866.

352 Shakspeare's Sonnets never before interpreted: his private Friends identified: together with A Recovered
Likeness of Himself. By Gerald Massey. 8vo, cloth,
uncut. London, 1866.

353 A Bibliographical and Critical Account of the Rarest
   Books in the English Language alphabetically arranged which during the last Fifty Years have come
   under the Observation of J. Payne Collier, F. S. A.
   4 vols., crown 8vo, cloth, uncut.   New York, 1866.
   In this American Reprint, the "Additions, Notes and Corrections" of
   the English edition have been inserted in their proper places, as foot-notes.

354 The Mad Folk of Shakespeare.   Psychological Essays.
   By John Charles Bucknill, M. D.   Second Edition,
   Revised.   Small 8vo, cloth, uncut, new.
                        London and Cambridge, 1867.

355 Shakspere: Some Notes on his Character and Writings.
   By a Student [E. Forsyth].   8vo, half morocco, uncut.
                        Edinburgh, 1867.

356 Shakespeare Illustrated by Old Authors By William
   Lowes Rushton.   2 vols., 12mo, cloth, uncut.
                        London, 1867-8.

357 On Early English Pronunciation, with especial reference
   to Shakspere and Chaucer. . . . By Alexander J. Ellis,
   F. R. S.   Parts I.–IV.   4 vols., 8vo, original wrappers,
   uncut.   London, 1867-74.

358 A Catalogue of the Books, Manuscripts, Works of Art,
   Antiquities, and Relics, illustrative of the Life and
   Works of Shakespeare, and of the History of Strat-
   ford-upon-Avon; which are preserved in the Shake-
   speare Library and Museum in Henley Street.   [By
   Clarence Hopper.]   8vo, cloth, uncut.   London, 1868.
   " 'Here is the cate-log.' Two Gentlemen of Verona, III. i. Joseph Cros-
   by, from Sam. Timmins."

359 A Dictionary of the Language of Shakspeare.   By
   Swynfen Jervis.   Royal 8vo, cloth, uncut.
                        London, 1868.
   .   The author of this valuable work died while it was passing through the
   press. The publication of the last half was superintended by Mr. Alexander Dyce.

360 Human Life in Shakespeare. By Henry Giles. Small
8vo, cloth, gilt top. Boston, 1868.
Lectures before the Lowell Institute.

361 An Introduction to the Philosophy of Shakespeare's
Sonnets. By Richard Simpson. Crown 8vo, cloth.
London, 1868.

362 Familiar Quotations: being an Attempt to trace to their
source Passages and Phrases in Common Use. By
John Bartlett. Fifth Edition. Crown 8vo, cloth.
Boston, 1868.
Pages 17-135 are occupied with quotations from Shakespeare.

363 The English of Shakespeare; illustrated in A Philological
Commentary on his Julius Cæsar. By George L.
Craik. Edited, from the Third Revised London Edi-
tion, by W. J. Rolfe. Crown 8vo, half morocco, brown
edges. Boston, 1868.
A few marginal notes by Mr. Crosby.

364 English Reprints. Edited by Edward Arber. 30 parts
bound in 8 vols., foolscap 8vo, half red morocco, gilt
tops, rough edges. London, 1868-70.
A complete set of these well-known and highly valued Reprints.

365 Shakspeareana Genealogica. Part I. Identification of
the Dramatis Personæ in Shakspeare's Historical
Plays: . . . Notes on Characters in Macbeth and Hamlet. . . . Part II. The Shakspeare and Arden Families,
and their Connections: with Tables of Descent. Compiled by George Russell French. 8vo, half morocco,
uncut. London and Cambridge, 1869.
Uniform in size and binding with the "Cambridge Shakespeare." See No.
68.

366 The Shakspeare Treasury of Wisdom and Knowledge
By Charles W. Stearns, M. D. 12mo, cloth.
New York, 1869.

367 The Autograph of William Shakespeare, with Fac Similes
of his Signature as appended to various Legal Docu-

5

ments; together with 4000 Ways of Spelling the Name
according to English Orthography. By George Wise.
4to, cloth.   Philadelphia, 1869.

368 A Hand-Book of Reference and Quotation. Mottoes &
Aphorisms from Shakspeare: arranged alphabetically,
with a copious Index of Words and Ideas. Post 8vo,
cloth, red edges.   Philadelphia (London), 1870.

369 The Bibliographer's Manual of English Literature. . . .
By William Thomas Lowndes. New Edition, Revised,
Corrected and Enlarged . . . . By Henry G. Bohn. 6
vols., 8vo, half roxburghe, gilt top, uncut.
                                  New York (London), 1869.
LARGE PAPER. Only 100 copies printed for America, No. 35. Pages
2253-2366 are devoted to Shakespeare. "Gives an amazing amount of detail
about all the editions of Shakespeare's works, with collations, prices, &c."—
Sam: Timmins, 1885. Comes down to 1864.

370 A Critical Dictionary of English Literature and British
and American Authors Living and Deceased from the
the earliest accounts to the latter half of the Nineteenth
Century . . . . By S. Austin Allibone. 3 vols., royal
8vo, half turkey morocco, marbled edges.
                                          Philadelphia, 1870.
Fine copy. Pp. 2006-2054 devoted to Shakespeare. Inserted is an autograph letter from the author to Mr. Crosby, dated Nov. 22, 1872.

371 A Shakespearian Grammar. An Attempt to Illustrate
some of the Differences between Elizabethan and
Modern English. For the Use of Schools.. By E. A.
Abbott. Revised and Enlarged Edition. Crown 8vo,
half morocco, brown edges.   London, 1870.

372 The Sonnets of Shakespeare Solved, and the Mystery of
his Friendship, Love, and Rivalry revealed. Illustrated
by numerous Extracts from the Poet's Works, Contem-
porary Writers, and other Authors, By Henry Brown.
8vo, cloth, uncut.   London, 1870.

373 Shakespeare and the Emblem Writers; an Exposition
of their Similarities of Thought and Expression.

Preceded by a View of Emblem-Literature down to A.
D. 1616. By Henry Green. With numerous Illustra-
tive Devices from the Original Authors. *Portrait.*
Royal 8vo, cloth, gilt, uncut.   London, 1870.
A handsome volume full of curious learning.

374 Among My Books. By James Russell Lowell. Crown
8vo, cloth.   Boston, 1870.
First Edition. "Shakespeare Once More," pp. 151-227.

375 Representative Men: Seven Lectures. By. R. W. Emer-
son. Small 8vo, cloth.   Boston, 1870.
"Shakspeare; or, the Poet," pp. 185-216.

376 Lectures on the Literature of the Age of Elizabeth, and
Characters of Shakespear's Plays By William Hazlitt.
Crown 8vo, half calf, gilt, marbled edges.
London, 1870.

377 Notes and Conjectural Emendations of certain Doubtful
Passages in Shakespeare's Plays. By P. A. Daniel.
Small 8vo, cloth, uncut.   London, 1870.
Inserted is an autograph letter from the Author to Mr. Crosby.

378 The Method of Shakespeare as an Artist, deduced from
an Analysis of his leading Tragedies and Comedies.
By Henry I. Ruggles. Small 8vo, cloth.
New York, 1870.

379 Prof. O. Phelps Brown's Shakespearian Almanac. Seven
in 1 vol., 16mo, half calf, marbled edges.   1870–76.
The same. 1877–80. 4 in one bundle. To be sold as
one lot.

380 Shakespeare's Euphuism. By William Lowes Rushton.
12mo, cloth.   London, 1871.
"Nearly 150 passages of Shakespeare traced in part to 'Euphues.'"

381 Shaksperean Fly-Leaves and Jottings, A new and enlarged Edition, by H. T. Hall. Post 8vo, cloth.
London, 1871.

382 A Collection of Lithographic Facsimiles of Early Quarto
Editions. 9 pp. 8vo, paper. London, 1871.
Publisher's descriptive list.

383 Shakespeariana. A Collection of Books, Pamphlets, etc.,
illustrating the Life and Writings of Shakespeare.
50 pp. 8vo, paper. London: A. R. Smith, Nov. 1871.

384 Shakspeariana from 1564 to 1864. An Account of the
Shakspearian Literature of England, Germany, France
and other European Countries during Three Centuries,
with Bibliographical Introductions by Franz Thimm.
Second Edition Containing the Literature from 1864
to 1871. 8vo, paper covers. London, 1872.
Some additions, in manuscript, by Mr. Crosby.

385 Shakspere and Typography; being an attempt to show
Shakspere's Personal Connection with, and Technical
Knowledge of, the Art of Printing. Also, Remarks
upon some common Typographical Errors, with espe-
cial Reference to the Text of Shakspere. By William
Blades. 8vo, cloth, uncut. London, 1872.

386 The Concordance to Shakespeare's Poems: An Index to
every Word therein contained By Mrs Horace Howard Furness Venus and Adonis 8vo, original wrappers. Philadelphia, 1872.
A trial instalment of the Concordance to all the Poems. See No. 304.

387 Two Dissertations on the Hamlet of Saxo Grammaticus
and of Shakespear. I. The Historical Personality of
Hamlet. II. The Relation of the 'Hamlet' of Shakespear to the German play, 'Prinz Hamlet aus Däne-
mark,' etc. By R. G. Latham. 8vo, cloth, uncut.
London, 1872.
Part I. is reprinted from the Transactions of the Royal Society of Literature, Vol. X., New Series.

388 Shakespeare: His Life, Art, and Characters. With an
Historical Sketch of the Origin and Growth of the

Drama in England. By the Rev. H. N. Hudson. 2
vols., 8vo, half turkey morocco, gilt top, uncut. Fine
copy. Boston, 1872.

389 Catalogue of the Shakespeare Memorial Library, Birmingham.. By J. D. Mullins. Three parts bound in
one volume, 8vo, half morocco, red top.
Birmingham, 1872-76.

Describes upwards of Four Thousand Volumes of English Editions and
Shakespeariana. The English portion only had been printed, when, in 1879,
almost the entire collection, of upwards of Seven Thousand Volumes, was
destroyed by fire.

"The most original and valuable Shakespeare Catalogue yet produced
. . . Merely as a record of Shakespeare editions and literature, it deserves
the highest praise as a volume of enduring and increasing value."—*Sam:
Timmins*, 1885.

390 Caliban: the Missing Link. By Daniel Wilson, LL. D.
Crown 8vo, cloth, uncut. London, 1873.

A few pencil notes in margins by Mr. Crosby.

" A comparison between this Caliban of Shakespeare's creation, and the
so-called ' brute-progenitor of man' of our latest school of science."—
Preface.

391 The Still Lion. An Essay towards The Restoration of
Shakespeare's Text. By C. M. Ingleby, LL. D. Reprinted, with additions, from the Second Annual Volume of the German Shakespeare Society. 8vo, limp
cloth. London, 1874.

392 Trilogy. Conversations between Three Friends on the
Emendations of Shakespeare's Text contained in Mr.
Collier's Corrected Folio, 1632, and employed by recent
Editors of the Poet's Works. [By J. Payne Collier.]
Printed for Private Circulation Only. 3 parts in 1
vol., 4to, half morocco, red top, uncut. Uniform with
Collier's Edition of Shakespeare of 1878. See No. 91.
London, [1874.]

VERY SCARCE. "Twenty-five copies printed . . . . The object of this
little work was to point out how Dyce, Singer, and other editors have made
use of the emendations while abusing the emendator."—*Henry B. Wheatley*.

393 Essays on Shakespeare By Karl Elze, Ph. D. Translated with the Author's Sanction by L. Dora Schmitz.
8vo, cloth, uncut. London, 1874.

394 A Concordance to Shakespeare's Poems: An Index to
every Word therein contained By Mrs Horace Howard Furness Royal 8vo, cloth, uncut.
Philadelphia, 1874.
Follows the text of the Cambridge Edition.

395 The Succession of Shakspere's Works and the use of
Metrical Tests in settling it, &c. Being the Introduc-
tion to Professor Gervinus's 'Commentaries on Shak-
spere' translated by Miss Bunnètt . . . . By Fredk. J.
Furnivall. 8vo, paper covers. (2 copies.)
London, 1874.

396 Shakespeare's Centurie of Prayse; being Materials for a
History of Opinion on Shakespeare and his Works,
Culled from Writers of the first Century after his
Rise . . . . . [By C. M. Ingleby.] 4to, paper covers,
uncut. London, 1874.
First Edition. Beautifully printed, in antique style, on Whatman paper,
large margins. "Of the deepest interest throughout."—*Joseph Crosby.*

397 The Philosophy of "Hamlet." By Thomas Tyler. 32
pp. 8vo, limp cloth. London, 1874.
Holds that Hamlet's madness was feigned and that his philosophy is
pessimistic.

398 The Confessions of. William Henry Ireland containing
the Particulars of his Fabrication of the Shakspeare
Manuscripts; together with Anecdotes and Opinions
of many distinguished persons in the Literary, Politi-
cal, and Theatrical World. A New Edition with an
Introduction by Richard Grant White. . . . *Facsimiles.*
8vo, cloth, uncut. New York, 1874.
The original edition appeared in 1805.

399 Shakespeare-Lexicon. A Complete Dictionary of all the
English Words, Phrases and Constructions in the
Works of the Poet. By Dr. Alexander Schmidt. 2
vols., royal 8vo, half morocco, gilt edges. ,
Berlin and London, 1874–75.
Paged continuously, 1452 pp. "One of the most learned, accurate, and
valuable works of our day."—*Sam: Timmins.*

400 A Select Collection of Old English Plays. Originally
published by Robert Dodsley in the year 1744. Fourth
Edition, now first chronologically arranged, revised and
enlarged, with the notes of all the commentators, and
new notes by W. Carew Hazlitt. 15 vols., crown 8vo,
cloth, uncut, new.   London, 1874–76.

> " Not only has the editor brought together, and arr nged in their proper
> sequence, certain dramas of great curiosity hitherto not reprinted at all,
> but he has incorporated with the old series of Dodsley all the pieces in the
> collections of Dilke, Hawkins, &c , which still remain uncollected."—*Note
> to Preface.*

401 PUBLICATIONS OF THE NEW SHAKSPERE SOCIETY. 35
parts, 4to, original wrappers, uncut, new.
                                                London, 1874–84.

> Complete from the beginning to 1882 inclusive, except Cromo-foto-lithograf
> and Platinotype, issued in 1881 and 1882, (Series VI, Nos. 9, 10); also, 2 parts
> for 1884.

402 The New Shaksperian Dictionary of Quotations. (With
Marginal Classification and Reference.) By G. Som-
ers Bellamy. . . . 8vo, cloth.   London, 1875.

403 Shakespeare Commentaries By Dr. G. G. Gervinus
Translated under the Author's Superintendence by F.
E. Bunnètt New Edition, Revised by the Translator.
Thick royal 8vo, cloth, uncut.
                                          New York (London), 1875.

> Contains an Introduction of 32 pages, by F. J. Furnivall, on the succes-
> sion of the plays, etc.

404 Fairy Tales Legends and Romances illustrating Shakespeare and other Early English Writers. [Edited by
W. C. Hazlitt.] To which are prefixed Two Preliminary Dissertations 1. On Pigmies 2. On Fairies By
Joseph Ritson. Crown 8vo, boards, uncut.
                                                London, 1875.

405 A Study of Hamlet. By Frank A. Marshall. 8vo, cloth,
uncut.   London, 1875.

> " Its views of Hamlet's character and other questions are for the most
> part sensible and sound."—*The Athenæum.*

406 The Romance of the English Stage. By Percy Fitzgerald, F. S. A. 12mo, cloth. Philadelphia, 1875.

407 The Authorship of Shakespeare. By Nathaniel Holmes. Third Edition. With an Appendix of additional matters, including a notice of the recently discovered Northumberland MSS. 8vo, cloth. New York, 1875.
An elaborate production in advocacy of the "Bacon-Shakespeare-craze."

408 Shakespeare's Library   A Collection of the Plays Romances Novels Poems and Histories employed by Shakespeare in the Composition of his Works   With Introductions and Notes   Second Edition   Carefully Revised and greatly Enlarged   The Text now First formed from a New Collation of the Original Copies [Edited by W. C. Hazlitt.] 6 vols., crown 8vo, boards, uncut. London, 1875.
" Probably embraces within its limits all that will ever reach us in the shape of Shakespeare's sources of information."—*Preface.*

409 The Western. Small 8vo, half morocco, marbled edges. St. Louis, 1875.
No. for June, 1874, bound in. Articles on Shakespeare by D. J. Snider and W. T. Harris.

410 Shakespeare's Plutarch   Being a Selection from the Lives in North's Plutarch which illustrate Shakespeare's Plays. Edited with a Preface, Notes, Index of Names, and Glossarial Index   By the Rev. Walter W. Skeat, M. A. Crown 8vo, red cloth, uncut. London, 1875.

411 Macready's Reminiscences, and Selections from his Diaries and Letters. Edited By Sir Frederick Pollock, Bart. Crown 8vo, cloth. New York, 1875.

412 A History of English Dramatic Literature to the Death of Queen Anne   By Adolphus William Ward. 2 vols., 8vo, half red morocco, gilt tops, uncut. Fine copy. London, 1875.
A work of great interest and value. Inserted is an autograph letter from the author to Mr. Crosby.

413 Hamlet; or, Shakespeare's Philosophy of History. A
Study of the Spiritual Soul and Unity of Hamlet. By
Mercade. 8vo, limp cloth. London, 1875.
" The wildest extravagance of German speculation upon the remote sig-
nification of Shakspeare seems tame beside this attempt to solve the mys-
tery of ' Hamlet '."—*The Athenæum.*

414 Shakspeare Diversions A Medley of Motley Wear
By Francis Jacox [First and Second Series.] 2 vols.,
8vo, cloth, uncut. London, 1875–77.

415 The English of Shakespeare; illustrated in A Philological
Commentary on his Julius Cæsar. By George L.
Craik. Edited by W. J. Rolfe. Eighth Edition.
Small 8vo, cloth. Boston, 1876.

416 An American Shakespeare-Bibliography by Karl Knortz.
12mo, paper. Boston, [1876].

417 Shakespeare Manual. By F. G. Fleay, M. A. Post 8vo,
8vo, red cloth. London, 1876.
Must be used with caution on account of the author's insistence upon the
great importance of Metrical Tests.

418 Wit, Humor, and Shakspeare. Twelve Essays. By John
Weiss. Crown, 8vo, cloth. Boston, 1876.

419 Shakspeare's Dramatic Art. History and Character of
Shakspeare's Plays. By Dr. Hermann Ulrici. Translated from the Third Edition of the German, with Additions and Corrections by the Author. By L. Dora
Schmitz. 2 vols., crown 8vo, cloth, uncut.
London, 1876.
" He is the real chief of the later school of German Shakspere-critics,
the key-note to whose system is the internal evolution of literary progress,
and, in reference to the individual genius of Shakspere, the conviction that
each of his works has a fundamental idea, so that together they form a har-
monious and self-complementary whole."—*A. W. Ward.*

420 Shakespeare Scenes and Characters. A Series of Illus-
trations. Designed by Adamo, Hofmann, Makart,
Pecht, Schwoerer, and Speiss; Engraved on Steel by
Bankel, Bauer, Goldberg, Raab, and Schmidt. With

Explanatory Text selected and arranged by Professor
E. Dowden. Small folio, cloth, gilt edges.

London, 1876.

421 Papers on Shakspere. By Robert Cartwright, M. D. 45
pp. 8vo, original wrappers. London, 1877.

422 Falstaff's Letters By James White Originally published in 1796 and now reprinted verbatim et literatim
With Notices of the Author collected from Charles
Lamb Leigh Hunt and other contemporaries. 12mo,
cloth, uncut. London, 1877.
"A bundle of the sharpest, queerest, profoundest humours of any these
juice-drained latter times have spawned."—*Charles Lamb.*

423 Shakespeare, from an American Point of View; including an Inquiry as to his Religious Faith, and his
Knowledge of Law: with the Baconian Theory considered. By George Wilkes. 8vo, cloth, uncut.

London, 1877.
First appeared in Wilkes's "Spirit of the Times."

424 Collins' School and College Classics. Introduction to
Shakespearian Study. By F. G. Fleay. Foolscap 8vo,
cloth. London and Glasgow, 1877.
A safer guide than the "Manual." See No. 417.

425 Shakespeare's Home; visited and described by Wash-
ington Irving and F. W. Fairholt: with a Letter from
Stratford by J. F. Sabin: and the Complete Prose
Works of Shakespeare. With Etchings by J. F. and
W. W. Sabin. 8vo, cloth, gilt top, uncut.

New York, 1877.

426 Literature Primers. Edited by John Richard Green, M.
A. Shakspere. By Edward Dowden, LL. D. 16mo,
cloth. London, 1877.

427 System of Shakespeare's Dramas. By Denton J. Snider.
2 vols., crown 8vo, cloth, uncut. St. Louis, 1877.
"From the Author. Dec. 20, 1877."

428 Literature Primers. Edited by John Richard Green,
M. A. English Literature by the Rev. Stopford
Brooke, M. A. Fourth Edition. 16mo, cloth.

London, 1877.

429 *Another copy.* New Edition, Revised and Corrected.
16mo, cloth. London, 1880.

430 Shakespeare The Man and The Book: Being a Collection of Occasional Papers on the Bard and his Writings. Part the First. By C. M. Ingleby.

London, 1877.

Occasional Papers On Shakespeare: Being the Second
Part of Shakespeare the Man and the Book. By C.
M. Ingleby. London, 1880.

2 vols., 4to, boards, uncut.

431 Studies on the Text of Shakespeare: With numerous
Emendations. And Appendices. By John Bulloch.
Crown 8vo, cloth, uncut. London, 1878.

" As usual in such cases, some good, some bad, some indifferent."—*Joseph
Crosby.*

432 The School of Shakspere ... Edited, With Introduc-
tions and Notes, and an Account of Robert Greene, his
Prose Works, and his Quarrels with Shakspere. By
Richard Simpson. 2 vols., crown 8vo, cloth, uncut.

London, 1878.

"Mr. Simpson's account of Robert Greene and his prose works is the best
I know. . . . . However any reader or critic may differ with Mr. Simpson's
views, I feel sure that he will hold these volumes a most useful and valuable
contribution to the knowledge of the Elizabethan stage and time."—*F. J.
Furnivall.*

433 New Readings & New Renderings of Shakespeare's
Tragedies By Henry Halford Vaughan 2 vols., 8vo,
cloth, uncut. London, 1878-81.

" His notes are rather improvements than amendments, and conse-
quently all wrong. We do not want a Shakespeare *improved*; we want
Shakespeare as he *wrote himself* only."—*Joseph Crosby.*

434 An Attempt to Determine the Chronological Order of
Shakespeare's Plays. The Harness Essay, 1877. By
the Rev. Henry Paine Stokes. Post 8vo, red cloth.
London, 1878.
A useful and scholarly work.

435 Shakespeare : Did he Write the Works attributed to
Him? By Charles C. Cattell. Third Edition, with
Notes on "What Shakespeare learnt at School." 16
pp., paper. London, [1878?].

436 Catalogue of the Works of William Shakespeare, Original and Translated. Barton Collection, Boston Public
Library. By James Mascarene Hubbard.
Boston, 1878.
Catalogue of Works relating to William Shakespeare and
his Writings in the Barton Collection, Boston Public
Library. By James Mascarene Hubbard.
Boston, 1880.
Two parts bound in 1 vol., imperial 8vo, half morocco,
red top, uncut.
200 copies printed. 227 closely printed pages in double columns, containing
2401 numbered titles and thousands of cross references. The alphabetical
arrangement of the Shakespeariana renders the contents easily accessible.
Truly " an important contribution to Shakespearian literature."

437 A Sketch of Shakespeare. By William Leighton. 8vo.,
cloth, gilt edges. Wheeling, 1879.

438 Bibliotheca Dramatica et Curiosa. Catalogue of the Library of J. H. V. Arnold, sold by Leavitt & Co., April,
1879. 8vo, paper covers, uncut. New York, 1879.

439 Mr. Swinburne's "Flat Burglary" on Shakspere. Two
Letters from the "Spectator" of September 6th and
13th, 1879. By F. J. Furnivall. A leaflet of 4 pages.
London, 1879.

440 The Shakespeare Key: Unlocking the Treasures of his
Style, elucidating the Peculiarities of his Construction,
and displaying the Beauties of his Expression; form-

ing a Companion to "The Complete Concordance to Shakespeare." By Charles and Mary Cowden Clarke. Thick 8vo, half morocco, sprinkled edges.

London, 1879.

441 Shakespeare's Centurie of Prayse; being Materials for a History of Opinion on Shakespeare and his Works, A. D. 1591–1693. By C. M. Ingleby, LL. D. Second Edition, Revised, with many Additions. By Lucy Toulmin Smith. 4to, half morocco, gilt top, uncut.

London, 1879.

LARGE PAPER. "This copy, being No. 23, of twenty-six large-paper copies issued (whereof No. 26 was found imperfect) of Shakespeare's Centurie of Prayse, by C. M. Ingleby, LL. D. is presented to Mr. Joseph Crosby of Zanesville, Ohio, by his sincere friend the author. March, 1880."—*Mr. Ingleby's autograph inscription.* See No. 396.

442 Memoranda on the Tragedy of Hamlet. By J. O. Halliwell-Phillips, F. R. S. *Facsimiles.* 8vo, cloth, uncut.

London, 1879.

Privately printed, and SCARCE. Autograph letter of the author inserted, dated March. 1880.

"The more I read of the tragedy of Hamlet the less I really understand it as a whole, and now despair of meeting with any theories that will reconcile its perplexing inconsistencies."—*Preface.* Very suggestive, nevertheless.

443 Memoranda on All's Well that Ends Well, The Two Gentlemen of Verona, Much Ado about Nothing, and on Titus Andronicus. By J. O. Halliwell-Phillips, F. R. S. 8vo, cloth, uncut. Brighton, 1879.

"Joseph Crosby, Esq, Zanesville, Ohio, U. S. A. With the Author's kind regards. Hollingbury Copse, Brighton, England, July, 1881."—*Autograph inscription.* Inserted is an autograph letter from the author, dated May 26, 1881.

Privately printed, and SCARCE.

444 Memoranda on Love's Labour's Lost, King John, Othello, and on Romeo and Juliet. By J. O. Halliwell-Phillips, F. R. S. 8vo, cloth, uncut. London, 1879.

Autograph inscription as in preceding. Privately printed, and SCARCE.

445 Library of Harvard University. Bibliographical Contributions. Edited by Justin Winsor, Librarian. No. 2.

Shakespeare's Poems. A Bibliography of the Earlier Editions. By Justin Winsor. 9 pp. Cambridge, 1879. No. 10. Halliwelliana: A Bibliography of the Publications of James Orchard Halliwell-Phillips. By Justin Winsor. 30 pp.   Cambridge, 1881.

2 pieces, large 8vo, paper.

446 An Aid to Shakespearean Study. By John Jeremiah. *Chandos Portrait.* 8vo, boards.   London, 1880.

447 Elizabethan Demonology An Essay in Illustration of the Belief in the Existence of Devils, and the powers possessed by them, as it was generally held during the Period of The Reformation, and the times immediately succeeding; with special reference to Shakspere and his Works By Thomas Alfred Spalding. 8vo, cloth, uncut.   London, 1880.

448 Shakespeare and Classical Antiquity Greek and Latin Antiquity as presented in Shakespeare's Plays (Crowned by the French Academy) By Paul Stapfer Translated from the French by Emily J. Carey. 8vo, cloth, uncut.   London, 1880.

449 An Index to Shakespearian Thought : A Collection of Passages from the Plays and Poems of Shakespeare, classified under appropriate headings and alphabetically arranged by Cecil Arnold. 8vo, cloth.
London, 1880.

450 Shakespeare's Morals: Suggestive Selections, with brief collateral Readings and Scriptural References. Edited by Arthur Gilman. 12mo, cloth, gilt top.
New York, 1880.

451 Shakspeare's Knowledge and Use of the Bible. By Charles Wordsworth, D. C. L., Bishop of St. Andrews. Third Edition with Appendix containing additional

Illustrations and Tercentenary Sermon. Crown 8vo, cloth, uncut. London, 1880.

452 A Study of Shakespeare By Algernon Charles Swinburne 12mo, cloth, uncut. New York, 1880.

453 The Stage or Recollections of Actors and Acting from an Experience of Fifty Years A Series of Dramatic Sketches By James E. Murdoch. *Etched Portrait on India Paper.* 8vo, cloth, uncut.
Philadelphia, 1880.
LARGE PAPER, NO. 113.

454 English in Schools: á Series of Essays. By Henry N. Hudson. 16mo, cloth. Boston, 1881.

455 *Another copy.* 16mo, cloth. Boston, 1881.

456 Shakespeare Prize Examination. 34 pp. 8vo, paper.
Hollins Institute, Va. 1881.

457 The Mystery of Hamlet. An Attempt to Solve an Old Problem. By Edward P. Vining. 12mo, cloth.
Philadelphia, 1881.
Contends that Hamlet's nature is "essentially feminine."

458 The England of Shakespeare. By Edwin Goadby. 16mo, paper covers. London, [1881].

459 The Literature of the Age of Elizabeth. By Edwin P. Whipple. Crown 8vo, cloth. Boston, 1881.
Originally delivered as lectures before the Lowell Institute in 1859.

460 The Shakespearean Myth William Shakespeare and Circumstantial Evidence By Appleton Morgan. Crown 8vo, cloth. Cincinnati, 1881.

461 The Shakespeare Phrase Book By John Bartlett. Crown 8vo, cloth. Boston, 1881.

462 The Library Magazine of American and Foreign Thought. Vol. VIII. 16mo, half russia. New York, 1881.
Contains a paper on "The Study of Shakespeare," by Joseph Crosby. Pp. 121-136.

463 Copy of Correspondence [between J.O. Halliwell-Phillips and Robert Browning]. 7 pp., folio. (3 copies.)
[Brighton, 1881.]

464 The "Co." of Pigsbrook & Co. [By F. J. Furnivall.] 6 pp. 8vo. (2 Issues.) London, 1881.

465 Reports of New Shakspere Society. A bundle.
London, 1881–84.

466 The Subjection of Hamlet: an Essay toward an Explanation of the Motives of Thought and Action of Shakespeare's Prince of Denmark. By William Leighton. With an Introduction by Joseph Crosby. 4to, cloth, gilt top, new. Philadelphia, 1882.

467 *The same*, cloth, gilt top. Philadelphia, 1882.

468 *The same*, cloth, gilt top. Philadelphia, 1882.

469 *The same*, cloth, gilt top. Philadelphia, 1882.

470 Familiar Quotations: Being an Attempt to trace to their sources Passages and Phrases in common Use. By John Bartlett. Eighth Edition. Crown 8vo, cloth.
Boston, 1882.

471 "On Massinger and The Two Noble Kinsmen." By Robert Boyle. Transactions of New Shakspere Society, 1882. pp. 371–399. 8vo, sewed.

472 Shakspere and Euphuism. By Dr. F. Landmann. Ditto, pp. 244–276. 8vo, sewed.

473 Was Hamlet Mad? By Dr. Brinsley Nicholson. Ditto, pp. 341–369. 8vo, sewed.

474 Prologue [to A. Y. L. I.] written and to be spoken by Mary Cowden-Clarke. Westwood House, July 5, 1882. 4 pp. 4to, sewed.

475 The Bibliography of the Bacon-Shakespeare Literature.
Compiled by W. H. Wyman. 8 pp. Small 4to, half
morocco, red edges, neat.   [Cincinnati, 1882.]
FIRST EDITION. LARGE PAPER.

475* *The same.* Small 4to, sewed.   [First Edition, large
paper.   Cincinnati, 1882.]

476 Some Shakespearean Commentators   Appleton Morgan
Crown 8vo, paper covers. 80 pp.   Cincinnati, 1882.

477 University of Michigan   Shakespeare Course   References for the Use of Students   By Isaac N. Demmon.
16 pp. 16mo, paper covers.   Ann Arbor, 1882.

478 Notes upon some of Shakespeare's Plays   By Frances
Anne Kemble . . . . 8vo, cloth, uncut. London, 1882.
Beautifully printed in brown ink.

479 Outlines of the Life of Shakespeare.   By J. O. Halliwell-
Phillips, F. R. S. The Second Edition. Thick 8vo,
cloth, uncut.   London, 1882.
"Subtle and gratuitous assumptions of unsupported possibilities will be
rigidly excluded, and no conjectures admitted that are not practically re-
moved out of that category by being in themselves reasonable inferences
from concurrent facts."—*Extract from Preface.*

480 Ward and Lock's Illustrated guide to Birmingham.
16mo, boards.   London, [1882?].
Excursion to Stratford, pp. 87 and following.

481 Spennel's Family Almanac, Directory of South Warwickshire, and Annual Advertiser for 1883. 8vo, limp
cloth.   Warwick, [1883].

481* Shakspeare's Birthplace.   An Artist's Pilgrimage to
Stratford-upon-Avon. By F. N. Shepherd, Esq. 16
pp. 16mo, sewed.   London, n. d.

482 Two Shakespeare Examinations: with some Remarks on
the Class-Room Study of Shakespeare. By William
Taylor Thom. 16mo, cloth.   Boston, 1883.
Presentation copy from the author to Mr. Crosby.

6

483 *The same.* 16mo, cloth.   Boston, 1883.

484 *The same.* 16mo, cloth.   Boston, 1883.

485 Shakespearean Relics. The History of Shakespeare's
     Brooch. Reprinted from the Stratford-upon-Avon
     Herald, April 13th, 1883. With Additions.
                              Stratford-upon-Avon, 1883.

486 Cruces Shakespearianæ Difficult Passages in the Works
     of Shakespeare The Text of The Folio and Quartos
     Collated with the Lections of recent Editions and the
     old Commentators With original Emendations and
     Notes By Benjamin Gott Kinnear. Small 8vo, cloth,
     uncut.   London, 1883.

487 Shakespeare's Bones. The Proposal to Disinter them,
     considered in relation to their possible bearing on his
     Portraiture: Illustrated by instances of Visits of the
     Living to the Dead. By C. M. Ingleby, LL. D. 4to,
     boards, uncut.   London, 1883.
       Advocates disinterment.

488 Outlines of the Life of Shakespeare. By J. O. Halliwell-
     Phillips, F. R. S. The Third Edition. Thick 8vo,
     half crimson levant morocco, gilt top, uncut. Fine
     copy.   London, 1883.
       See No. 479.

489 Shakespeare as a Lawyer By Franklin Fiske Heard
     Small 4to, white cloth, gilt top.   Boston, 1883.

490 Medical Thoughts of Shakespeare. Compiled by B.
     Rush Field, M. D. 16 pp. 8vo, sewed.
                              Easton, Pa., 1884.

491 "O Poor Ophelia." By Miss Grace Latham. Transac-
     tions of New Shakespere Society, 1884. pp. 401–430.

492 Folk-Lore of Shakespeare By the Rev T. F. Thiselton
     Dyer. 8vo, cloth.   New York, 1884.

493 Rolfe *versus* Hudson. 8 pp. [2 Issues.]
[Cambridge, 1884.]

494 Corrigenda and Explanations of the Text of Shakspere.
By George Gould. A New Issue, showing hundreds
of Mistakes existing in the Standard Editions of the
Plays of the Great Dramatist. 64 pp. 8vo, limp cloth.
London, 1884.

495 The *Ἅπαξ λεγόμενα* in Shakspere. By James D. Butler.
14 pp. 8vo, sewed. [2 copies.] Madison, Wis., n. d.

496 *Shakespearian Magazines.* 1 vol., 8vo, half morocco,
marbled edges.

> Contains : *Macmillan's,* March 1875, "On the Motive of Shakspere's
> Sonnets"; *The Galaxy,* April 1875, "The Tale of the Forest of Arden";
> *Lippincott's,* April 1875, "On the Study of Shakespeare's Sonnets"; and
> three others.

497 *Ditto.* 1 vol., 8vo, half morocco, marbled edges.

> Contains: *London Quarterly,* January 1859, Review of Dyce's First Edi-
> tion, 16 pp.; Ditto, July 1871, "Shakespeare," 26 pp.; *Edin. Rev.,* April 1856,
> "The Corrector of Shakspeare," 14 pp.; Ditto, July 1869, "Shakspearian
> Glossaries," 18 pp.; Ditto, Oct. 1872, "New Shakspearian Interpretations,"
> 20 pp.

498 *Ditto.* 1 vol., 8vo, half morocco, marbled edges.

> Contains: *Gentleman's Magazine,* April 1875, "In Shakespeare's Coun-
> try;" *The Cornhill,* Nov. 1875, "Shakspere's 'Macbeth' and another;" Ditto,
> Feb'y 1867, "Shakspeare's Greek Names;" and others.

499 Eclectic Magazine, New Series, Vol. I. 8vo, half morocco,
marbled edges. New York, 1865.

> "Hamlet," pp. 455–473. "A well-written, judicious, masterly article and
> merits attention."—*Joseph Crosby.*

500 Atlantic Monthly. 8 numbers, containing articles on
Shakespeare and the Elizabethans, by Whipple, R. G.
White, and Mrs. F. A. Kemble. 1 vol., 8vo, half
morocco, marbled edges. [Boston, 1859–1868.]

501 *Shakespearian Magazines.* 1 vol., half morocco, marbled edges.

> Contains: *The Fortnightly,* May 1875 and Jan. 1876—Swinburne's "The
> Three Stages of Shakespeare;" *Scribner's,* April 1875 and Sept. 1875, "The
> Shakespeare-Bacon Controversy" and "A Study of Shakespeare's Portraits."

502 *Shakespearian Miscellany.* 1 vol., 8vo, half morocco,
marbled edges.

Contains: Frederickson's Review of Hamilton, New York, 1860; Wilkie
Collins's Shakespearian Novel, "The Stolen Mask" (Peterson's Ed.); and
several others enumerated on inside of cover.

503 The Church Eclectic. 9 numbers, containing articles
on Shakspeare, by the' Rev. J. A. Bolles, of Cleve-
land, Ohio. Utica, N. Y., 1879–80.

504 Shakespeariana. 21 numbers, many duplicates.
Philadelphia, 1883–4.

505 Bundle of English Magazines containing articles on
Shakespeare: Blackwoods, The Cornhill, Macmillan's
Temple Bar, St. James's, etc. 11 in all. London, v. d.

506 Another: Nineteenth Century, Frazer's, The Gentleman's Magazine. 16 numbers in all. London, v. d.

507 Bundle of American Magazines containing articles on
Shakespeare. The Atlantic, Galaxy, Manhattan, and
Century. 18 numbers in all.

508 Another: Scribner's, Appleton's. 14 numbers.

509 Sabin's American Bibliopolist. Vol. I–IV, complete. 4
vols., half roan. New York, 1869–72.

510 *Ditto.* Vol. IV. half morocco, marbled edges.

511 *Ditto.* Vols. V. and VI. in one vol., half morocco, marbled edges. New York, 1873–74.

Lacks last 4 numbers of Vol. V.

512 *Ditto.* Vols. VII. and VIII. 2 vols., half morocco, marbled edges. New York, 1875–76.

Shakespearian Gossip, conducted by J. Parker Norris. Many contributions thereto by Mr. Crosby.

513 The Antiquary. 4to. 4 odd numbers, containing Shakespeariana. Also, The Bibliographer, No. 1, 1881. To
be sold as one lot.

514 The Academy. A Weekly Review of Literature, Science, and Art. March, 28, 1874 (No. 99) to August 13, 1881 (No. 484) inclusive, complete. 4to, original numbers. 15 lots. London, 1874–81.
Vols. VI. to XIX. inclusive, and parts of V. and XX.

515 The Athenæum Journal of English and Foreign Literature, Science, the Fine Arts, Music and the Drama. Jan. 7, 1871 (No. 2254) to March 21, 1874 (No. 2421) inclusive, except No. 2316 missing. Also 11 odd numbers. 4to, original numbers. 7 lots. London, 1871–81.
Both the above contain much Shakespearian matter.

516 NOTES AND QUERIES. First and Second Series Complete. 24 vols., with the RARE INDEXES; in all 26 vols., small 4to, cloth, uncut. London, 1850–61.

517 *The same*, for the years 1866, 1868, 1873–1883 inclusive. 26 vols. complete, and 25 odd numbers (no duplicates), all in the original numbers. London, 1866–84.
These volumes abound in matter of interest to Shakespearian students.

IV. WORKS OF OTHER DRAMATISTS.

518 The Works of Sir William D'Avenant. Consisting of Those which were formerly Printed, and Those which he designed for the Press: Now published out of the Author's Originall Copies. Folio, old calf.
London, 1673.
Lacks Portrait.

519 Beaumont and Fletcher. Fifty Comedies and Tragedies. All in one Volume. Published by the Author's Original Copies, the Songs to each Play being added. Folio, old calf, red edges. London, 1679.

520 William Wycherley. Plays. 12mo, old calf.
London, 1731.
Contains, The Plain Dealer, The Country Wife, Gentleman Dancing Master, Love in a Wood.

521 The Plays of Philip Massinger, in Four Volumes. With Notes Critical and Explanatory, By W. Gifford, Esq. The Second Edition. *Portrait (water-stained).* 4 vols., 8vo, half crimson morocco, gilt tops, uncut.
London, 1813.
Fine copy of the BEST EDITION.

522 The Works of Ben Jonson in Nine Volumes. With Notes Critical and Explanatory, and a Biographical Memoir, By W. Grifford, Esq. 9 vols, 8vo, full calf, marbled edges. London, 1816.
Still the favorite edition.

523 The Works of Beaumont and Fletcher; the Text formed from a new collation of the early Editions. With Notes and a Biographical Memoir by the Rev. Alexander Dyce. 11 vols., 8vo, tree calf, gilt, marbled edges, by ANDREW GRIEVE, Edinburgh. London, 1843-46.
A superb copy of the best edition. SCARCE.

524 The Dramatic Works of Richard Brinsley Sheridan. With a Short Account of his Life. By G. G. S. *Portrait.* Crown 8vo, cloth, uncut.
London: Bohn. 1848.

525 The Works of John Marston. Reprinted from the Original Editions. With Notes, and some Account of his Life and Writings. By J. O. Halliwell, F. R. S. F. S. A. 3 vols., small 8vo, half calf, marbled edges. Fine copy. London, 1856.

526 Modern Standard Drama. 5 vols., 12mo, half roan. Eight Plays in each volume. New York, v. d.
A collection of Acting Plays.

527 The Dramatic and Poetic Works of Robert Greene and George Peele. With Memoirs of the Authors, and

Notes, by the Rev. Alexander Dyce. 8vo, half morocco, gilt top. London, 1861.

528 Dramatic Works of Wycherley, Congreve, Vanbrugh, and
Farquhar. With Biographical and Critical Notices,
by Leigh Hunt. A New Edition. *Frontispiece and
vignette.* 8vo, half morocco, gilt top, uncut.
London, 1866.

529 Dramatic Works of Massinger and Ford. With an Introduction, by Hartley Coleridge. A New Edition.
Portrait and . vignette. 8vo, half morocco, gilt top,
uncut. London, 1869.

530 The Works of John Ford, with Notes Critical and Explanatory by William Gifford, Esq. A New Edition,
Carefully Revised, with Additions to the Text and to
the Notes by the Rev. Alexander Dyce. 3 vols., crown
8vo, cloth, uncut. London, 1869.

531 The Works of Christopher Marlowe : With some Account of the Author, and Notes, by the Rev. Alexander
Dyce. A New Edition, Revised and Corrected. 8vo,
half morocco, gilt top. London, 1870.

532 The Works of John Webster : With some Account of
the Author, and Notes, by the Rev. Alexander Dyce.
A New Edition, Revised and Corrected. 8vo, half
morocco, gilt top. London, 1871.

533 The Dramatic Works of Richard Brome containing
Fifteen Comedies now First Collected 3 vols., 8vo,
boards, uncut. London, 1873.
LARGE PAPER COPY, published at Three Guineas.

534 The Comedies and Tragedies of George Chapman now
First Collected with Illustrative Notes and a Memoir
of the Author. 3 vols., small 8vo, boards, uncut.
London, 1873.

535 The Plays and Poems of Henry Glapthorne now First Collected with Illustrative Notes and a Memoir of the Author. 2 vols., small 8vo, boards, uncut.

London, 1874.

536 The Dramatic Works of Thomas Heywood now First Collected with Illustrative Notes and a Memoir of the Author. 6 vols., small 8vo, boards, uncut.

London, 1884.

"Heywood is a sort of *prose* Shakspeare. His scenes are to the full as natural and affecting. But we miss *the Poet*, that which in Shakspeare always appears out and above the surface of *the nature.*"—*Charles Lamb.*

537 Every Man in his Humour. By Ben Jonson. With Introduction and Notes, by H. B. Wheatley. 16mo, cloth. London, 1877.

538 Tragedy of Doctor Faustus. By Christopher Marlowe. With Introduction and Notes, by Wilhelm Wagner. 16mo, cloth. London, 1877.

539 Marlowe's Tragedy of Edward the Second. With Introductory Remarks ; Explanatory, Grammatical, and Philological Notes ; etc. By F. G. Fleay. Foolscap 8vo, cloth. London and Glasgow, 1877.

540 The Sons of Godwin. A Tragedy. By William Leighton, Jr. 16mo, cloth, gilt top. Philadelphia, 1877.

541 At the Court of King Edwin. A Drama. By William Leighton, Jr. 16mo, cloth, gilt top.

Philadelphia, 1878.

542 Marlowe's Doctor Faustus and Greene's Friar Bacon and Friar Bungay. Edited by Adolphus William Ward. Foolscap, 8vo, cloth. Oxford, 1878.

543 Marlowe's Edward the Second. Edited by Osborne William Tancock. Foolscap, 8vo, cloth. Oxford, 1879.

+

www.ingramcontent.com/pod-product-compliance
Lightning Source LLC
Chambersburg PA
CBHW020037030726
47499CB00007B/2466